# Spirit2Priest

## Shaikh Tauqir Ishaq

شيخ توقير إسحاق

"Spirit Priest 2"

ISBN 978-0-9575442-6-0

Published by Shaikh Tauqir Ishaq

251015 hti
www.spiritpriest.com

*This Book is dedicated to all those who serve*

*Bismillaah…*

# Contents

# 1.   A Battered Heart

A difficult beginning.  The young man was confused, a little excited and nervous all at the same time.  His Reticular Formation working at full speed allowing him to experience all these emotions together.  His thinking struggling to keep pace as there was so many possibilities to consider.

"So," asked the Priest, "What do you think?"

He was in a very confused state.  Unable to decide what to do and what the consequences would be.  He was totally oblivious to the golden autumn sunshine which he had been admiring earlier, whilst driving to the Priests office.  There were a few people walking around outside braving the chill to catch the last decent rays of sun before the inevitable freezing rains and then the bleak, bitter, miserable winter.

"Should we start now?" he asked, with his voice shaking slightly.

The Priest paused.  There was nothing he would have liked better than to encourage him, but, he knew it wouldn't be easy.  "It will take some time," he replied, "because your memories when you were six will not easily revive themselves.  We are talking about over twenty years ago.  Some have been completely forgotten."

"But...is… is she alive?  And what about my brothers?"

The Priest deliberated further.  He spoke softly to him.  "Look," he began, "I think it's best that you start searching.

Let's see what happens after that. Let's have no expectations. It's been a long time."

Then the *salaams* and good-byes, leaving the young man in deep thought and contemplation. He even walked passed his car he was so distracted and had to remind himself exactly where it was. (Although to be honest, not a make or model to boast about.)

That evening his search began. A young refugee when he first came to the UK. A lost little boy at the mercy of a difficult and ruthless world. He used to sweep train carriages in India with his two elder brothers for fractions of coins to look after their widowed mother.

Now he was all grown up. Tall, toned, well educated with a good job and yet yearned to find his lost and forgotten family. They had told him at the orphanage that they were all dead, just so they could sell him. As he was very sweet looking with wide, lovely brown eyes, they would get a good price. And sell him they did. His foster parents finally admitted to him they were sure the Orphanage director had lied to them and that he was not an orphan at all. They were desperate to adopt him so believed everything they were told at that time.

So the search was on. This huge question mark above his head for so long could now begin to be addressed. He knew that when he had fallen asleep he had slept for around two hours. Then he travelled for another three hours before reaching the large city of Nagpur, central India where he joined three million other people. Not knowing where his brothers were, he had searched the train but to no avail. They had in turn thought he had got off the train as a quick search failed to find his little body rolled up in the corner of a seat.

So the train pulled into this large, unfamiliar and busy metropolis. He did not know this place and was forced to leave the train by the strict duty guards. It was night time and he was scared. His brothers had always drummed into him how he should look after himself. Not to trust strangers, to always keep a look out for the police and officials and to avoid them. The train staff just shooed him away and out of the station as he was just another obscure professional beggar. They ignored his pleas to get back on another train returning to where this one came from. But it was hopeless. Now he was now out and on his own in unfamiliar territory. All strange, confusing and intimidating.

He tried to stay near the station but was threatened by the local beggars who fiercely protected their patches. One of them beat him and so he had to run. Now living on the streets, he begged for money and a few kind shop keepers used to give him food. For three months he lived like an urban wild animal - a human fox - not knowing when or where his next meal was coming from and getting shelter where he could. Only six years of age, relying on wit, instinct, innocence and the charity of others to survive. One can only try and imagine his predicament and never be able to imagine it.

Numerous times people tried to lure him into a dangerous and exploitative world, but due to his training, he just ran. Eventually though the police had a crackdown, arrested him and placed him in an orphanage. There he was groomed and eventually sold to a good family. This family had previously been advised by the Priest to adopt such a child some months before. Now this same adopted young man was receiving guidance from the very same Priest. How blessed are the silent spiritual eddies guiding the sincere to goodness. These wondrous currents are life's secret and sacred forces of righteousness.

So the search was afoot, using just a few scraps of his unreliable memory. Satellite imagery of India had just been completed and was available free online. He remembered the railway station, the stream they used to play in and a small lake. He had also worked out a rough distance he had travelled but did not remember the name of his village, except the local slang name they called it. He had no idea though how accurate it was as he couldn't find the name anywhere from the search engines. When he was six he couldn't read, so he was not able to recall the name of the train station or village or much else.

He started having dreams about his mum and his village and it was at this time his foster parents encouraged him to meet the Priest. Now the tense search had begun. There were little snippets of memory he would have to rely on. A siding at the station for example and a local stream, but who knows what had changed? It was a rural village then, but what about now? He focused on the raw infrastructure. The stream had to still be there and so should the lake and railway station. However, he wasn't prepared for the length of time this would take. It was a monumental challenge.

One month searching and still nothing. Sometimes he hunted all night and at other times he just gave up after a few minutes. It was frustrating and it was tedious. The nervousness and excitement had been replaced by monotony and disappointment. He had tried to establish a system of searching but failed the first few weeks, until he found some software that was able to track where he had searched. He tried to find all the lakes but then realised that possibly his recollection was in error and it may have been not been a 'lake', rather a small pond - one that simply filled up when it rained. The perspective of a child is far different to that of an adult. The search was stressful and it was slow. Long and laborious hours of futility. He never appreciated before how weak and temporary memories could be.

Then, one evening, after some thirteen weeks of searching, this dreary-eyed, tired, overwhelmed young man was scrolling across some images of a small stream not too far from a series of rocks acting like a weir. There was also an enormous pipe going across the stream and a railway line not too far. He continued to move the cursor over some fields and then quickly sat up alert as he hurriedly scrolled back, impatient for the image to update itself. He peered closely at the screen. This looked a little familiar and also a little unfamiliar. He panned around the area trying to visualise what it would look like from the ground. He then followed the railway line to the station and saw a siding with some carriages on it. The buildings were all extremely unfamiliar as he was seeing them from the air. He then moved the image back to the stream, which appeared to open up downstream of the weir. 'Could this be a potentially large pond?' He zoomed in and poked around a little more. There was a little cliff possibly where they used to dive from. He didn't really recognise it, as there seemed to be a new wall and hand railings there. Clearly health and safety had finally caught up in this rural area.

But it looked so different...and there were also some striking similarities. He was desperately probing his childhood memories, but it was so long, long ago. Was this the place or was his mind playing tricks? His desperation and imagination mixing to confuse him.

He traced the route from the stream to the train station. One which he followed almost every day for two years. It just looked so different. He didn't recognise the route or the landmarks. Then he remembered something along the train track. When they set off, they always passed a large level crossing and then the train crossed a bridge over the stream. They used to sometimes throw stones out of the windows, seeing who could hit a particularly large rock in the stream. This gave people time to settle down before they offered their cleaning services. And there it was. A bridge, with the twisting stream flowing underneath it's path.

He zoomed out and sat back in state of denial and disbelief. His mind was racing. Decisions were being explored, their various branches and consequences assessed and then plans were being made and then un-made. What if it was the wrong village? What has happened to his mother? His brothers? Should he travel there? Should he not? What if they were all dead? What if they were alive? What if they didn't remember him? What...what...what...?

Exhausted, he fell asleep thinking, worrying, contemplating. He dreamt of going to a village. It was a cloudy dream, foggy, fuzzy and confusing. Then a clarity. A clearness. Sanity. A wondrous feeling. The Priest was suddenly standing in this village with his broad, reassuring smile, appearing relaxed and looking around, bringing calmness to the panic. The clouds were clearing and the fog disappearing. He was still smiling as he faded with the mist, busy with people.

In the morning, the young man told his foster parents what had happened. He told them that he had phoned the Priest and had asked his guidance and permission to go to India and to search. He had also been advised to do so.

The travel arrangements were made very quickly. He had continuously checked the imagery of this village to try and remind himself but just became more familiar with it rather than being reminded. It had been far too long.

The flight was painfully slow and the economy seats just pathetic and painful. However, the advice he had taken form the Priest before leaving made it easier. His holy beads being read and the thought that his mother and brothers may be alive and well and still in the village. The Priest had advised him to go and that said a lot to him. Then the train ride to his village. The most heart-rendering sight to bear were the beggars and the intense poverty, and the offer of small children begging to clean his carriage. Then cleaning it anyway to make him obliged. That was him, an immense lifetime ago. No big deal for him, he was just giving away pennies, but pounds for the children. They are what he was, all those years ago and his emotions were all jumbled and confused.

The time had come. The train was pulling into the station. His whole body began to tremble (and it wasn't the diarrhoea this time). Slowly, the diesel engine braked as the train grudgingly slowed down with squeeches, squeals and scrapes. It did not appear to want to stop and shuddered and jolted as it negotiated some points. The station slowly came into view as the train reluctantly slowed. Various people now began to approach the carriages. A few beggars, passengers, sales people - all previously hiding in the shadows trying to protect themselves from the scorching might of the sun. Although it was late afternoon, it was still shining brightly like a furnace, baking the roasted landscape. Then the train stopped with a loud bang. He didn't want to get off and he did want to get off. Like a zombie he got up, surprised at how many of the passengers were actually departing. He grabbed his shoulder bag and traversed his way passed all the boxes, bags, babies, legs, and rubbish. He was out; standing; looking around. But nothing. No reminders, no memories, no sudden gain of lost time. It all looked weird and unfamiliar. Just the normal, strange rural India with the chaotic smells, confusing sights and curious locals. A dusty, smelly and muddled scene lay before him.

He left the station and walked out onto a dust covered track. He met a Rickshaw driver and asked how much to the waterfall and pipe going across the river. He only had a vague idea which direction to go, but he felt totally lost, completely alone and extremely unsettled. The rickshaw driver was totally oblivious to the massive frenzied and emotional madness the young man was experiencing. He was just focused on getting ten times what he would normally charge. The young man just nodded when the exorbitant price was offered as he was too troubled to deal with such trivial and mundane matters.

The rickshaw motor started up and its rough, single piston engine spluttered and whined as it propelled the vehicle along the bouncy, dusty track. Horses, cows, chickens, children, motorcycles, trucks and other rickshaws were all using this confused transport artery. Not very crowded, but completely disorganised to the untrained eye and with the rule 'might is right'. The driver appeared to know all the deep potholes as did everyone else, all fighting for the flattest sections and strips of track. He had hoped for a refreshing cool breeze but got a blast of oven-hot air as the three-wheeler bumped and bounced along.

After some ten minutes of joggles, shakes and being battered by the inside bars of the rickshaw, it choked to a halt in front of a house. No movement any more. Bliss. The driver turned off the engine and mumbled that there was no road to the river, but that he could go down this alley. The young man was in a daze. This alley looked strange but also familiar. He was still not used to the strong smell of dung always wafting whether freshly deposited or being dried and burned. The billions of flies were definitely used to it and happily attempted to transfer bits of the droppings onto humans. At this time they all appeared to be after him.

He paid the driver who was confused as to why this well dressed tourist would want to come here. He did ask as the young man was leaving but got the answer that he was meeting someone. The rickshaw drove off bouncing up and down on the track as the young man started his walk of optimism, anticipation and hope. He was breathing fast and was on full alert. He couldn't take breaths that were too deep because of the raw odours and the hot, dry air. However, he was practically gliding, slowly through the alley. Dusty, dark, dirty and smelly. Open drains with the occasional toxic fluid. Disgusting. Wild cats and dogs half asleep but half alert, all thin, hot and panting. Too hot to sleep and too hot to move.

After a few minutes he heard the sound of water and then he saw it over a wall. It wasn't a waterfall, rather a few rapids in a small stream. But there was the proud pipe crossing the stream in a giant, elongated 'n' shape. Rusted, with graffiti and patched with welds some thirty metres away. He decided to climb over the wall, which had obviously been built to stop flooding. With difficulty he scaled the hot, dusty, dirty structure and found himself on the banks of this stream. Not as clean as he had expected and very shallow. In fact looking more like a large drain with bits of plastic and other rubbish slowly floating past and other pieces trapped between stones. A small lizard-like creature was resting in the shade, frozen in the heat, almost totally camouflaged by his surroundings. A small statue almost hidden under a small rock.

It all looked so different, but it was all in the right place. The station, stream, pipe, rapids...it was all there. A lost childhood in plain view. A jigsaw of his history slowly being assembled but still with the most important pieces missing.

He was standing in the sun, with sweat dripping down his face and drenching his shirt. His head was hurting slightly. He was looking at the few children brave enough to be playing in the water. An old man was watching him, sitting on the floor under a makeshift asbestos roof. It was made up of various items with bits and pieces sticking out and with an old material draped over the top. It looked flimsy and weak just like the old man. He didn't want to move but was curious as to the young man's expression and strange, hot attire. Totally out of place but with a look of want and desperation behind one of upset and confusion. He moved his old bones into a squatting position and with a groan got himself up. With his hand supporting his lower back, he began to walk towards this young man. Slowly, and more with will-power than with his muscles he reached him and spoke to him in the village dialect. Being surprised that he understood and could speak a little.

"What do you want?" he asked.

"I want to know..." he answered, "I want to know if this is my village."

"Don't be silly, this is not for city folk. You sound like you are from abroad anyway from Amreeca, not here."

The young man looked at this old man's darkened, weary face. He was tired but peaceful. Accepting his age and position. Just watching life go by and his own life pass. Just then he caught a whiff of exceptionally strong dung and scrunched up his nose. The old man though appeared unaffected.

"I grew up here I think," answered the young man trying not to cough.

"Then you shouldn't have come back," he responded almost immediately.

"My family could be here," he answered as he coughed a little, trying to get the stench out of his nostrils and mouth.

The old man just watched him unperturbed. When the young man had settled a little, he then continued the dialogue: "Who are you?"

"I used to clean train carriages with my brothers," he answered, "some 25 years ago and I got lost."

The old man paused. His old brain begun to work and then found an excuse to stop working.

"I've been here all my life," he said, "and I don't know you. And I know everyone. You're in the wrong place"

"It was 25 years ago," he replied again. "Please... could you help me? I need to know whether any of my family is here or not."

"What were their names and what did you used to do?"

The young man repeated that he used to clean carriages and mentioned his brother's nick-names. The old man then began to breathe deeply as his brain was once again activated. It took him a full minute before he was able to say something.

"Yes," he said. "Yes. You went missing and then your brothers went missing. Yes...yes."

There was a shocked pause. Brothers? He mentioned his brothers? He must know.

"Do you remember me?" he asked.

"No, no," said the old man, "but I do remember three children who worked together cleaning carriages for their mother. Then the youngest went missing and a few months later so did the other two. It was very sad and it was very bad. It was a long time ago. They are all dead." With that the old man struggled to sit on the wall that the young man had previously jumped over. He helped him sit.

He smelled of an old, musty odour. He had very few remaining teeth and sat down with a painful gasp. He had exhausted himself by overusing his brain and extracting some deep, deep memories, very old and obscure. But had retrieved enough. Now he was tired.

There was a pause. The young man had been told by the Priest that there will be people who would remember him. Was it this old man? It must be.

"So..." he began, but couldn't finish the sentence as the old man interrupted him.

"Are you the youngest?" asked the old man, "or the eldest?"

"The youngest," the young man replied now sighing deeply. He was definitely getting somewhere, but where was this going?

"Hmmm," the old man sighed.

13

"So, my...my mum?" asked the young man. "Is she..ermmm.. errr… well…. h-here?"

"Hmmm," replied the old man. "Yes, I think she's around somewhere." A pause. "Help me up, I will take you."

This was shocking. Before he had time to think and absorb the answer the old man was trying to get up and obviously needed assistance. His thin, malnourished, bony body slowly becoming upright. Then they both began to walk. This now seemed a little recognisable. Through some back alleys, around the corner and there it was. A familiar shaped house and front door. It surely can't be the same house? But it looked like it was. This was just too much. He was being led by the old man straight towards this small, unassuming door, behind which....?

The old man then lifted up his thin, bony arm and tapped on the door, shouting something in slang. There was a pause and then a shuffling sound from inside. He shouted something again. After a little while, the door opened slowly and it opened completely. There stood an extremely old and fragile woman. Dressed in dulled clothes and a loosely fitted scarf. Barefoot, tired but brave-faced. Weary eyes, dimly lit with faded hope. Her heart had been battered by the events in her life, events deserving of no one, but her enduring spirit had survived.

She looked at the old man and quickly glanced at the young man, then looked at the old man again. All were quiet. Nothing was said and nothing was meant to be said. The eyes did all the talking. The young man was looking at this small, wrinkled and lonely face in front of him and now she was looking back at him, both desperately trying to determine and to reason and to work something out. A precious and priceless moment in time. All emotions were paused and trapped and refused to be released.

Minds were racing and time itself had slowed to a crawl as the past began to catch up with the present. It was a long, long stare. Her expression was one of confusion. Then disbelief. Then a fear. And now a slow and careful realisation as she slowly raised her fragile hand. It was trembling and fearful as it reached out to gently touch her son's head. She hesitated, but slowly moved her hand closer, shaking with trepidation and fear. Fear of being wrong and fear of being right. She slowly reached out and softly touched her son's head. Stroking it gently. Silenced by a whirlwind of emotion now beginning to be released. The young man was still staring. This woman was from a different world to his, but could this be his mum? Is this where he was from?

With incredible love and tremulous emotion she continued to stroke the side of his head. As he felt her touch his inner most being told him that it was sincere and it was genuine. Her other hand instinctively reached up as she now gently held his precious and priceless head with both her quivering arms. Her legs also were becoming weak, but she had to stand. She remembered every ache and every hurting of him being lost. Every day without him and not knowing was torture. She remembered every pain of his birth. She remembered all of his features. It was him, no matter how old he was, no matter how tall, no matter how beautiful and how splendid. A Priest had told her that her youngest was still alive and that he would return, but time had faded her hopes. And now, in front of her those words proving true.  She saw and recognised the shape of his head, his facial features.  And yes, he looked so much like her late husband.  She softly said his name and came closer to him with her old, fragile, trembling body.  A hopelessness, loneliness and emptiness for so many years.  A quarter of a century of tragedy and torture.  The painful circle now finally closed.  Emotions stored up for so long they had almost disappeared, but now they were fresh, raw and uncontained.  Released as relief, elation and ecstasy.  A deserving joy and a wondrous new existence as she finally embraced him and her tears mingled with his.

# 2.   *The Apprentice*

"School can teach you a lot," explained the Priest, "but it cannot teach you everything."

His student was sitting opposite in a maroon, Italian-style chair, made in the Far East. The Priest was sat in a high-backed cream-coloured chair in his small office. This young student had already displayed extraordinary qualities and been directed to the Priest who had begun mentoring him. Today the subject was knowledge and the question the Priest asked was basic, direct and unmistakeable.

"What is knowledge?"

The eager student replied immediately. "Something to know and understand," he replied. "Information," he added.

There was a pause. This student had a lot to learn. It was a typical and unwelcome response. Not worthy of where he was sat and whom he was trying to become. He answered too enthusiastically, too rashly and too inaccurately. His thinking and understanding were deep but his answers shallow. Life's answers cannot be found in a dictionary, they can only be found through wisdom and insight. This young man will need a number of tests and these had already been arranged and had begun. The Priest looked at his student, deeply but calmly, touching his heart with gentle direction.

The rain suddenly splattered against the window as a gust of wind decided to blow against it. It had been drizzling down for the past hour but the wind had picked up a bit. It was quiet outside as it was a dark, dreary, autumn night. Unwelcoming streets were all soaked, deserted and lifeless, while the office was comfortable, calm and peaceful. The four walls were surrounded by amazing books of knowledge from the floor to the ceiling. However, this was not just a room where only the books boasted knowledge. The master and protagonist of scholarship himself was sitting in front of this young student, enthusing learning and inspiring wisdom with every action and every word.

"No," said the Priest in response to the students answer. He had to humble this young man, more than he realised and more than he was prepared for. "It is far simpler than that and far more profound. It is enlightenment," he declared, "...of the heart, mind, soul and of others around you. It is factual and empirical at the most basic level. But it is enrichment of ones being at the higher levels. Only true knowledge has true impact and only true knowledge produces true change."

There was a brief pause and then the student, clearly eager to speak, blurted out, "Yes, it is something intangible, I understand."

The Priest looked at him with a slightly amused look. Impressed with his innocence, immaturity and eagerness. He was indeed spiritually very sensitive, full of potential but still required much time and effort. He had to be slowed down and made to realise that while youth is defined by impatience, maturity is defined by calmness. The Priest inhaled a deep, serene breath. He looked at the young man in-front of him and smiled warmly. "You should leave now," he instructed calmly.

He then added in a very soft voice, "And I'm not sure if I will call you back."

The student was shocked. "Has my training finished?" he enquired. "Have I failed?"

The Priest waited a little before answering. "No. Your training has yet to begin. Now please leave."

## 3.  The Body Builder

His bulging biceps were on display through the tight T-shirt.
As winter had just arrived, most had decided to wear warm,
light coats but mandatory muscles must be on show - especially
these ones.  The body builder was serious about pumping iron
and every muscle and vein boasted his pains and testosterone.
He was sat in the Priests office next to his mum.  In
comparison she was the opposite of body-building.  Small and
delicate, flimsy and frail.  Her son totally dominated the chair
he was sitting in which appeared to be doing well in supporting
his bulky upper body.

"How can I help?" asked the Priest.

Today was a surgery day and visitors were piled up outside
in the large lounge.  It was mid-morning and the son and his
mother had come especially early so that they would not need
to wait too long.  The body builder had sacrificed his morning
sessions of mind over matter – essentially permitting lots of
pain to allow himself to bulge abnormally – in order to seek
help from the Priest.  The mum had come because she had
quite a few things to say as well.  She was also happy that he
wanted some guidance.  As a good mum, she was over-
protective, overly caring and overly advising.

"This is ridiculous," said the body builder.  "I just don't
know what to do.  I don't take this off anyone," he protested.

The Priest was calm.  He had seen this body builder grow up
and had advised his family for many years.  He had spiritually

nursed him through many difficulties with and without his knowledge. The mother was in touch at all the critical times and was immensely grateful for the help. She was told that he would come to see the Priest when he was good and ready but she was impatient. Now she was appreciative and amazed that this had happened. The Priest knew that the body builder, whilst being generally friendly and peaceful had a huge weakness. He would not allow himself or his family to be insulted in any way. This had led to a few incidences in his school and some on the street as well. Luckily he had survived them, both physically and legally. The Priest decided to follow the slow and easy route as this was the body builders first time in this session.

"Please explain," he enquired.

"Well," he began, "I just don't know how to handle this. It's unfair and I can't understand it. I'm being messed around, insulted, assaulted and....well....tortured. It's wrong and I need to know what to do."

The Priest smiled, ever so slightly. He decided to help the body builder along. "Why don't you call the police?" he asked.

The body builder suddenly looked up, directly at the Priest who was sitting content and calm in his adjustable chair. His breathing and demeanour, soothing and saintly. He expected this reaction. In fact he had extracted it. The body builders expression now one of protest and surprise. Then he realised from the Priest's subtle smile that he was just teasing him. So he also smiled widely, relieved a little as he relaxed into his chair - although there was not much more room to relax in to be

21

honest. His body was already being squeezed between the arms of his seat. The chair was really struggling. He looked down at his mum with love and upset, helplessness and respect. His Biceps boasting their presence and still firmly on display. Veins prominent and protruding. He was sitting in 'display mode'.

The mum now started to speak. "He's still my son," she commented, "and I am helping him. It is my duty as his mum."

"Yes of course," the Priest responded. "That is a good thing. One to be always respected."

"I can't take it anymore," protested the body builder again. "It's enough." He turned away, clearly distressed. His emotions now back in turbo mode.

Man is built from carbon and fused with a variety of emotions - an unlikely mix. This bizarre combination creating both a weakness and a strength. Carbon can be as tough as diamond or as weak as graphite. Emotions add life to this lifeless element causing it to shine brilliantly and brightly or to become dulled and fragile, forever swapping and changing. The body builder was exhibiting the qualities and subtleties of both. Tough and testosteronic on the outside but flimsy and frail on the inside.

"But you are so big and powerful," his mum started, "everybody respects you and is scared of you. They wouldn't dare say anything because they know your temper. But I'm your mum," she added. "I am here to guide you...I will say what I like, when I like and how I like." Her English was basic but very motherly. A tinge of an Asian accent, mixed with local inflections and dialect. She had certainly learned all the key phrases she needed to and she also knew how and when to use them.

"That's just it," he protested. If anyone says anything to me, I will shut them up. Always have and always will. "But when my mum has a go....and hits me....what am I meant to do? She treats me like a kid!"

He was quickly becoming quite emotional again. Yes, he took no nonsense off anyone and never had in his life, muscles or not. However, his mum was treating him like he was still a baby. Constantly giving 'advice and guidance'. Telling him to eat his breakfast properly, tidy his room, come back at a decent time etc. etc. "I don't know what to do or what to say," he concluded as he started breathing a little faster and more audibly.

"If he is naughty, I will smack his bottom," she said. "Because he is my son. And I don't care how much he has trained his bottom."

"See?" he cried out. "See what I mean? Now that can't be allowed!" He was visibly, upset and now breathing heavily. Ironic as well as his bottom was probably the least muscular, relatively speaking.

The Priest was watching and admiring the intense chemistry between these two. He saw beyond the shallow arguments and the childish frustrations. It was deeply touching. Let alone the amusement of his fragile mother trying to assault her son – and he reluctantly allowing it. The depth of love these two had for each other was to be admired. The no-nonsense body builder at a total loss. Any other male or female he just needed to growl at and they kept away. Or simply face them, firm and immovable. Match won. But his mother was having none of it. Her small body squared up to his. Shouted at him every now and again. Told him off. Even pulled his hair sometimes (when he was sitting down of course) to complain about his haircut. She threatened to go with him to the barbers on numerous occasions. That was indeed a vicious threat as it had massive social repercussions for the body builder. It was something he was not going to take lightly and he had uncomfortable visions of his mother ambushing him in the Barbers.

The Priest decided it was time to act. Time to show them the love they had for each other and also to give the body builder a key to the door he had unknowingly locked in his mind. Once opened, his problem would be solved and solved forever. This would be the precious gift the Priest would give these two, who were currently locking horns, not for domination, not even for justice, but due to their innocent and precious love.

"How many mothers do you have?" asked the Priest to the body builder.

"Of course, just the one," he responded. "Just one. All of us do. One." He was still agitated as his slightly nervous tone and repetition indicated.

The mother then opened her mouth to speak but the Priest gently shook his head to stop her saying anything.

"How many people do you allow to treat you in this way....like your mother does?"

"No one would dare," he said, sitting upright and now with a more serious and determined look on his face. Muscles tensing and bulging even more. Would the chair cope? "No one has been born yet who would get away with such a thing," he growled.

"Don't you think..." began the Priest, "that you should allow one person...and only one person in your life to treat you with this... pampering? Someone who can innocently and sweetly tell you off? Someone who wishes the best for you, but doesn't necessarily know how to express it. Someone who gave birth to you, so she would always be your mum and you would always be her son. Someone who is so used to guiding you that she is now in a habit which she finds difficult to leave – proving that she is a good mum. Tell me, isn't there room for such a person in your life?"

The Priest and the body builder were looking straight at each other. He had absorbed a little of what the Priest said as his mind whirled round. The mother again wanted to say something but she stopped herself, remembering the Priest's previous expression which indicated 'please....leave him to me'.

The Priest gave the body builder a few seconds to digest a little more and then he continued. "It is only embarrassing if you allow it to be embarrassing. Your friends would admire and learn rather than laugh. Because they will see your giant frame being pushed around by your sweet, little mum, and your smile showing love and respect whilst she does it. And also your answers showing the same while she tries to push you against a wall," he said smiling. "I have thousands of followers," he continued, "and have been blessed with the strength and ability to help whomsoever I can. But when I visit my mother, I am equally blessed when she tells me off or tells me to wear my coat because it's cold, she still asks if I have eaten properly. So, I am happy that she has been given this position in my life."

The body builder was practically in a hypnotic state whilst listening and looking at the Priest. This amazing personality sitting in front of him - a strange but warm individual, distant but friendly, powerful but compassionate, wise and sincere. His words penetrated his mind, settled into his heart and enlightened his soul. He suddenly felt empowered – to allow his mum to tell him off, to shout and scream at him and even to assault him and all would be okay. Even if his friends were around as witnesses, he could cope and come out a hero to be followed and admired rather than to be a figure of jest. 'Yes', he thought, 'yes,' it could work. The solution had appeared from the mist that his mind was immersed in. The door was being unlocked. He was becoming more enlightened as the emotional shroud over his heart gradually lifted. The confusion as to his reaction to her maternal conduct towards him was being clarified. Now he had realised and now it was clear. All he needed to do was to do nothing. Just accept it for what it was – a sincere affection and her heartfelt expression of motherhood.

The Priest added, "Mothers are treasures. They are precious gems. With great torment and difficulty did they bring their children into this world. Yet they can receive nothing as true recompense. This has to be corrected but cannot be corrected.

Their patience and dedication has to be rewarded by their children with patience and dedication in reciprocation. A truly unjust position that cannot be repaid by their offspring."

Only a small adjustment was required in the thinking of this body builder, but the consequences would be profound. His muscles were strong, powerful and well defined. Now his mind and psyche had to be toned and developed. In such ways are personalities strengthened, characters corrected and the most important lessons in life are learned and practised. In this regard, the Priest was a provider of solutions and a referee in the arena of conscience. A pure and welcome guiding light in a confused and darkened world.

# 4.   The Slappable Face

Not a good beginning.  The young man was being extremely rude to his father in his words, tone and body language.  The father looked extremely upset, almost in tears.  This was not how he had perceived fatherhood when he had first got married and he certainly didn't need this now with his daughter getting married.

It was the middle of winter and bitterly cold outside.  This marriage function had been arranged in a rush and the only convenient dates were now.  No-one complained as the hall was extremely warm and pleasant and there was nowhere else to go in the midst of this season.

However, this was a nightmare for the father.  His son was now too old to argue with or beat into submission, although that had never really been an option.  Every attempt the father had made to bridge the chasm that existed between them was rejected with scorn and animosity.  All the advice he had sought and tried had failed.  His family members had also got a little involved and had all failed.  Now he was being humiliated in front of the Priest and his son appeared to enjoy his father's embarrassment and discomfort.  His father was almost in tears and his son responded with just more hurtful and abusive language.  His hatred of his dad and humanity was deep.

The Priest had been watching this show now for a good three or four minutes.  They were in a private office adjacent to the wedding hall.  Incredible though it may seem, the boy's sister was getting married and he decided at this time to make a scene. The Bride was on her way, her father was stressed beyond belief and now this. Although the father was quite timid, he had just about managed to stop one of his brothers from giving his son a massive slap and then dragging him out of the hall by his hair to teach him his lesson which 'he would never forget'. Other members of the family had ushered the father and son into a side room that had been setup for prayers. The Priest had just arrived and had been asked to help. He was accompanied into this room with the father's youngest son as they joined the father and his abusive son. Luckily, most guests had not arrived yet, just a few members of close family had turned up to help in the arrangements.

The young man's tongue was in full swing, being obnoxious to his father and his entire family. The insults were not simple swear words. They were deeply personal and extremely offensive - an affront to all decency and self-respect. The second son looked helpless and the father a lamb to the slaughter. All four were standing and the Priest was paid little heed. After a few more abusive and disgusting sentences the Priest had heard enough. It hurt him to see a good man being humiliated and insulted so he decided to act.

His presence was powerful. He walked up to the father and held him by his shoulders, gently guiding him backwards to a chair. The father moved without any resistance and sat down. He was a person numbed, defeated and in retreat. He put his head in his hands, ashamed and hurt. The Priest then turned to the youngest son and asked him to leave, but he whispered, "Lock the door from the outside and don't worry. Only open it when we ask you to". The younger brother obediently did what he was told.  He was too young and immature to be able to deal with this.  The young man had carried on with his abuse but as his brother left the room and locked the door, he became silent.  'What was happening?'

The Priest was now standing between the young man and the locked door.  The young man assessed the situation, thought for the second and then decided to take on the Priest.  "You think I'm scared of you?  I don't know who you think you are but you better get away from that door because I'm leaving.  Don't think it being locked will stop me.  I will throw you out of the way and break it down."

The Priest was calm.  "I really don't care what you think," he replied, "but I am not going to move."

The young man thought for a few more seconds.  His head felt a little light and then heavy.  He paused a little as he tried to keep his balance.  The room looked as if it was moving.  Dizzy...dizzy...dizzy.  He then composed himself and made his decision.  He screamed and ran full force at the Priest, his fists flying in a mad, uncontrolled frenzied charge.  The Priest was ready.  He moved onto his back leg and to his right slightly, as his left hand blocked the son's right wrist as it was flung at his head.  His right hand was poised for additional defence but was not required.  Instead it was used to grab the boys collar as his left hand held the boys right wrist extremely tightly, forcing his right arm upwards.  He allowed the boys momentum to let him move forward and past.  The young man now found himself bent over and the Priest then twisted his right arm behind his back while holding tightly onto his wrist and pushing his neck down at the same time. The young man's right arm was now in a stress position and was being held very tightly, very securely and very painfully. Every movement of his body caused the pain to increase. However, the young man was not having this. He struggled and screamed using his legs as best he could, but he was being held so tightly that he found it difficult. The Priest then twisted the young man's right arm behind his back even more and bent his wrist in the same motion so forcing him to his knees, his head practically touching the floor. The Priest was kneeling right next to the young man's head with his torso bearing down onto the young man's back. He had in one, artistic movement, manoeuvred the young man's body around and forced him onto his knees, doubled over, while gracefully falling to his knees as well. Now the only limb that could move was the young man's left arm. But the Priest was on the opposite side and it could not reach him. The Priest's left elbow was over the young man's head to prevent it looking up but the pain in his arm was doing that job already.

The Priest pulled the young man's right arm a little more towards his neck. A muffled scream of pain was heard and then the prostrated and subdued pile of flesh shook and screamed in defiance. One limb in the correct pressure position was controlling the entire body. The Priest looked over at the father who had watched the events unfold. He smiled at him. The father was in a state of shock. He had been attacked already like this and one punch had knocked him out of the way. He was out of energy and out of ideas. Now his son was in prostration – a position of worship. How he had prayed for this, although not quite like he had imagined.

31

"I'm going to call the police on you…you ……" and a volley of swear words followed.

"I will call them first because you attacked me," responded the Priest very calmly. "You will answer to them and to me," he added. He then pulled the young man's arm a little more and a muffled scream and a long groan was heard. Then a few more swear words.

"Let me go you …." It was incredible how few swear words could be used so frequently and in such a combination.

"You want to be a man, so fight like one or be defeated like one," stated the Priest. "You are over 18 so you are in the adult world. This is my world you have stepped into." The Priest remained firm in his Hapkido hold of the young man. He then turned to the father and asked, "How are you feeling? Would you like some water?" The father's mouth opened but no sound came out. Probably the answer was a 'no'. He was a frozen statue. His jaw dropped even more as his eyes stared in disbelief.

The young man had calmed down a bit. The Priest had ensured he was breathing and not being choked and in this sense the continuous insults had confirmed his airways were clear. There was little movement possible now and more submission than resistance. The Priest released his hold slightly on the young man's arm and he appeared to relax and be relieved. A good sign.

"Let me go!"

"No."

Then another volley of swear words combined with abusive adjectives. The Priest tightened his grip again. This wild stallion was being broken and he needed to be. A muffled scream and the young man managed to wriggle his legs free from underneath himself and spread them behind him. The net result was that his whole body was now flat on the floor but still firmly held and controlled via his twisted arm. A bit easier to wriggle but when he did his arm was moved higher towards his neck and wrist bent further back. Now, ironically, a new twist. As his legs became outstretched, the Priest had grabbed the young man's left arm and joined them both in a stress position on his back. Double trouble. The hold had become even more secure and every movement even more painful. His right wrist was still also bent back against itself, adding to the immense pain.

The young man's head felt a little light and then heavy. He tried to keep his balance. The room looked as if it was moving. Dizzy...dizzy...dizzy. The Priest stood motionless, staring at the young man – standing between him and the door. The young man was standing and thinking whether to attack him or not.

"I really don't care what you think," replied the Priest, "but I will not move because I don't care about your rudeness. However, if you do go through the door – your Uncle is waiting to slap you in-front of everyone. We've locked the door to help you but I think everyone will enjoy the *tamasha* as your face gets slapped repeatedly – except you."

The young man observed the Priest. He was tall, powerful with wide and relaxed shoulders. He looked calm and unperturbed. In his head he had gone through a scenario of running and screaming at him with his fists flying. However, he felt that the Priest had already defeated him as his eyes were focused on the young man's heart and soul. His strength radiated around him like an impregnable outer shell. It shouted determination and power. As if ten men standing there, not one. Now the young man felt small and dominated. Images drifting into his mind of the Priest defeating him, restraining him. Twisting his arm behind his back. More images of him being slapped repeatedly around the face by his Uncle who wasn't particularly fit – but overweight and knowing how to use his overhanging curry belly – with everyone watching. This young man now needed a way out and the Priest gave it to him.

"I can speak to your Uncle if you wish," he said, "I'm sure I can persuade him."

The young man still static, but his mind thinking fast and furiously. He felt a slight pain in his arms and wrists and suddenly starting feeling physically weak. The room still looked as if it was moving, but slower.

"What do you think?" the Priest asked. "Being slapped or being helped. You choose."

The arrogance was still showing as he defiantly turned away from the Priest and towards his father who was wide eyed and horrified as to the position his son had found himself in. His father looked at the Priest and then he looked at the closed door as he heard a commotion outside. His son also instinctively turned towards the door. At this point, the Priest moved slightly to his left, inviting the young man to go past. "Please. Feel free," he said as he gestured towards the door. "Go get slapped. They are looking forward to it"

The young man stomped across the room and brushed past the Priest making sure he did not touch him but came as close as he dared. He reached out and grabbed the door handle and then stopped as someone started banging madly on the door. "Where is the *badtameez bacha*?" his Uncle shouted furiously through the solid, wooden door. Banging again and then more hullaballoo as people tried to calm him down. The young man stepped back in fear. No way out and no way back. He now had fear in his eyes as this was too close to home - or rather, his uncles hand too close to his face. Now he was the lamb, cornered, helpless and ready for slaughter. He looked up at the Priest whose demeanour had changed to that of a protector rather than a punisher. A strength to be relied on rather than fought against. He was too proud to say it so the Priest said it himself. Softly, calmly and persuasively

"Come," he said, "take a seat and I will calm your uncle down. But if you won't sit I won't be able to help. That's all I ask.

The young man paused and then walked slowly towards the empty chair near his father and sat down. He was now nervous and had had placed his arrogance to one side while his face was now depicting a pretend defiance. Survival of dignity and especially of one's body was now priority. He still felt a strange pain in his right arm and right wrist. Visions of being slapped and a combined, viscous curry belly attack didn't help.

It took the Priest almost half-an hour to calm everyone down, after which the wedding went ahead with most guests ignorant of what had happened and what could have been. The son stayed in the small room on his own. Once the proceedings were mostly over and guests were just trying in folly to ease their digestive systems with caffeine beverages, the Priest left the main hall to go and have a quite word with the young man. The only thing that prevented him from leaving the wedding or making trouble was the fact that he had never seen so many of his Uncles so angry. The Priests presence had also confused him. Taking on his father was easy but his Uncles were non-nonsense, traditional family men who rarely showed any anger but were not to be messed with when they did. The young man had rarely seen this side of them. Like uncontrollable wild animals, smelling blood, the sight of their younger brother being upset on this important day caused them to switch to 'protect mode' and 'beat him senseless mode'. They were ready to give him his lesson for life which was 'behave or be punished', meaning being humiliated and slapped repeatedly if necessary. Respecting ones elders would be forced out if it did not come voluntarily and no-one cared about the consequences.

"How are you young man?" asked the Priest quietly. They were now alone in the private office. A mixture of smells of garlic, cooked meat and *biryani*. Also a faint smell of wood polish from the dull shine of the wooden wall panelling and the musty dust from the carpet all confusing the senses.

"I'm okay I think," replied the young man. He had not enjoyed one minute of this function and had hardly eaten. He had a cold sweat around his back and neck and was terrified every time his uncles looked at him. The looks spoke loudly and clearly, disseminating visions of being beaten repeatedly and being beaten by a group. 'You can hide, but your face will be found and slapped', was the message portrayed by their eyes.

"Why do you hate your father so much?" asked the Priest.

What? A direct question. A question that pierced through all the confusion and upset. A question that struck directly at the core of his being. A missile of words directly aimed at the cause – and the missile hit its mark. For every door there is a key and the key to this man's whole upset was about to be turned in his forbidden door. He looked up at the Priest, his expression confused but curious, weary but wondering. He answered. "I don't know," he began, "I just do. He just doesn't understand. No-one does."

To anyone else this would have been the end of the discussion or the start of a downhill slide to depression. However, to the Priest this was a plea for help. And in the plea there was also the solution. The illness and medicine were both apparent. But the solution had to be enacted, and the medicine had to be administered. Then it needed time to digest, absorb and activate.

The Priest began with the first dose of healing. A tablet aimed not at his heart, but at his soul. "Who is your closest friend?" asked the Priest.

The boy thought for a few seconds and then answered. "No one. There is no-one. Everyone hates me and I don't trust anyone."

"But there must be someone," the Priest said softly. "There is someone in your life whom you speak to. Someone who listens to you."

"No," he said a little more forcefully and a little desperately this time. "I've told you and you are not listening either." Now he was saddened and upset and wanted to clam up, but the Priest was unperturbed. The medicine was still being absorbed. And it was about to activate. For this, there had to be silence. A period of reflection. The Priest waited patiently. Timing is everything. And now was the time.

"Do me a favour," asked the Priest.

"What?" asked the young man despondently. Not expecting anything as everyone had let him down and all were gunning for him. Family and friends.

"Let me ask you just to do one thing."

"What?" asked the young man, uncaringly.

"Read something for me. Something that few people realise can have a huge impact on themselves. Something which is a great secret but I'm willing to share if you allow me to."

"Okay," said the young man, "what is this amazing secret? And don't think I'm just going to accept it or do it."

"Okay," said the Priest, "I accept."

"What do you accept?"

"I accept your challenge."

The young man was confused. "What challenge?" he asked. "I haven't challenged you."

The Priest laughed. "I just wanted to get your attention," he said. "But it won't cost you anything to repeat a few sentences. Just a few minutes a day. And it will stop you feeling lonely, plus strengthen you from within."

The boy looked indifferent and disinterested. He was upset and lonely. And these feelings had penetrated deep into his soul, burdening his being. The Priest acknowledged and was smiling. A calm, pleasant and extremely peaceful smile. Not threatening nor intimidating at any level. Neutral and knowing. Serene and strong. Delicately whispering. Quietly inviting. Radiating tranquillity. An irresistible oasis in the despairing desert. A commanding hand now began to reach out to the young man. It was not a hand of help, but one of understanding.

The Priest reached into his heart and gently touched his soul. It was the lightest of contacts but had an incredible impact. For the briefest of moments but with the most lasting impressions. An Angelic cradle comforting a troubled, sensitive and lonely soul. And then it happened. The boy looked up. A look of curiosity and wonder. Of hurt and want. Of 'keep away' but 'I will stay'. Of 'I don't believe you have anything' but 'okay let's see what you have'.

"What?" he asked. "What shall I read?"

The medicine had activated and the healing had begun. A channel opened and a connection initiated. A sad, lonely, angry and fragile existence had begun a transformation. To be shaped by life's trials and tribulations. His impressionable soul —now a blank ingot, to be fashioned and forged by the Priest's hand. Now it could begin its most important journey.

The young man would remember this encounter and how over the years, the perceptive guiding light of the Priest saved him, helped him, understood him and corrected him.

All require to be guided but whom to choose from the many available guides, begging for followers? It is clear – the one who knows, and knows that he knows. He is the one. The silent diamond who does not need to show himself as he already shines clearly and brightly for those who wish to see. The one whose few words have huge meaning, whose simple instructions are life-changing, whose heart, mind and soul in harmony with Creator. He saves, helps and guides with every word, every breath, every heartbeat. He is the one and only the sincere can benefit from him. Lucky are those who do and unfortunate are those who do not. When one laughs, the world is always ready to laugh with you. However, when one cries, one always cries alone. For this reason such great men are sent and they comprehend.

"Can I ask a stupid question?" inquired the young man.

"Ask," smiled the Priest, "but please remember," he said softly, "there are no stupid questions, only stupid answers."

40

# 5.   *413*

"You are going on a very long journey and I pray it is a successful one." These were the parting words from the Priest before the passenger had left. He had sought prayers from him before leaving as was his habit and thought nothing of them.

Half way to New Zealand, a small amount of turbulence shook the plane. There was no reaction from the passengers, most of whom were sleeping. It was pitch black outside and long-haul flights take their toll.

Two male passengers were sitting next to each other, both half-awake and watching films on the small screen in front of them. Seats built for midgets and toilet cubicles designed to suffocate. Passengers seated, subdued, and practically anesthetised by cabin design. Fatigue and boredom had infected everyone who had become dulled and subdued by their environment. All had now accepted the fact that their fate was now completely tied into that of the plane. There was no option but to accept.

The two men were opposites. Although both were from London and had origins in Asia, one was deeply religious and the other was not. One would help others at every opportunity but the other would pick and choose. Normally choosing selfishness and service of oneself above others. He thought he had a good heart but the other always put himself down. Both enjoying Business Class. And then it happened. The films being watched began to flicker and one of the engines began to splutter. There was no turbulence, no screaming, no emergency. There was a loud bang as one of the oil pumps in the left engine overheated, siezed and exploded. The explosion was uncontained and ruptured the engine casing which in turn slammed into the underside of the wing. The fuel tank split, the fuel poured out and ignited and then within a few seconds the wing was torn apart as it exploded. A blinding flash as the plane became immersed in a slow motion, scorching fireball. Then everything went quiet and everything went blank and everything went white.

Two beautiful, beaming faces welcomed the good man. He felt warm, safe and secure. The slight headache he had was gone. No aches and pains, no confinement, no noise. Serene and peaceful. A lovely, refreshing smell of rose petals, perfectly balanced in strength and sweetness. The beaming faces were speaking to him. It was Arabic but understood as if in English. His natural tongue. Beautiful and sweet. Rich and pure. Alluring and attractive.

"Come out," were the words he heard as he felt himself leave his temporary world for another. It was smooth and effortless, pleasant and painless. With a slight feeling in his neck for a brief second and a refreshing final taste in his mouth, he had completely exited one existence and entered another. He now felt released but also helpless. He wanted to panic but was immediately comforted by those around him.

"Welcome good servant, most welcome."

He felt at peace. It was still him. The original him rather than a facsimile. He looked around. Through a faint mist below him, he saw balls of bright orange fire with a black sooty clouds swallowing each other up and engulfing the plane as it tumbled down towards the ocean in slow motion. He was just outside the plane as it exploded and fell out of the sky. But not important. No loud noise, no heat, no pain; as if he was in a 4-D film. Being part of the action but with the volume turned right down and a false reality surrounding him. The plane, its position and its condition, inconsequential. He was floating and rising with these two beautiful Angels looking caring and welcoming as if they knew him and wanted to be with him. He felt safe and strange, fresh and light, strong and young. Even comfortable and normal. No...better than normal.

Around him he saw other souls rising. Dozens and dozens, each with 2 figures of light. There were some 413 passengers and crew aboard the plane. He remembered one of the Stewardesses mentioning the number to some ground staff just before she closed the main door. That was the moment all became trapped into their shared destiny and this was the reason they were on the plane.

Some souls were beaming with joy and happiness shining with a beautiful light. Others looking upset, dark and scary. He glimpsed the man who was sitting next to him. Not next to him anymore but to his right and below him slightly. He looked distressed and scared. His soul, dim and ugly. The two Angels with him had dark and frightening expressions. He could also smell a pungent odour when he looked at him so turned away and the bad smell went. He then heard his name being pronounced and that of his father and his grandfather. He was being announced and welcomed, honoured and praised. Angels upon Angels began to gather and joined the ascent. A radiant plume of light now spiralling upwards as far as the eye could see. Hundreds of Angels singing, chanting, welcoming him. He felt honoured and happy. His soul began to shed tears of contentment and with each tear a great sense of relief, a refreshing fragrance and a beautiful bliss.

The plane was now a distant memory. This was all divine and serene. Amazingly peaceful. Free from his body his soul was shining and fragrant, attracting more beauty. He did not want this to end. The rising was extremely fast now although it did not seem it. There was something ahead. The procession was heading towards it, now full of thousands of Angels, all chanting, radiant and welcoming as if a special guest had arrived.

Now familiar faces. His grandparents looking young and beaming brightly. They had with them a small child who looked excited to see him. 'Abu', he cried as his grandmother released him and he ran through the beautiful space to meet him. He gave him a massive hug. It was physical and it was real. The man recognised him even though he had not seen him for over 20 years. It was his son who died when he was just a few days old. He looked happy and well. Excited to see his father. The good man was crying. This was all so natural and all so unexpected. The deceased grandparents followed and greeted him with beautiful hugs. All smelled delightfully sweet and their souls, warm and refreshing and solid. Then Uncles, Aunties, great grandparents – dozens of people, all of whom he knew. There were others in the background but he didn't know them and they stayed back, all looking happy and peaceful, young and healthy.

"It is your time daddy," said the small boy as his grandmother took him back. They were fast approaching something which was vast. Left and right there was no end in sight. It extended into other dimensions which were covered in a fine mist so only faint glimpses were possible.

Then he heard his name announced along with his father's name. A beautiful, powerful and authoritative voice. A lovely glowing Angel emerged with a beautiful, large, golden bound book. It was decorated in a very special, celestial pattern that seemed to change with every angle, glowing with different colours and designs. Mystical and exquisite, scented and radiant, effervescing with goodness. The procession had stopped and there were vast lands all around populated by communities of pure Angels and souls. There were also large gates and walls surrounding even greater and more beautiful places but although he could not see beyond, his instinct had informed him.

The book was presented to him in his right hand. It energised him as soon as he touched it and its cover's beauty was astonishing and magical. His name was embroidered in gold thread and studded with glistening diamonds, radiating colours he had never before seen. The pages incredibly thin and fragrant with gold edgings, every word hand stitched and adorned in Arabic but all totally understandable. It was his life. Every word he had spoken, every action he had done. The good deeds were glowing and decorated and highlighted with silk and gold thread, exquisite diamonds and emeralds for the small dots in the words. The bad deeds were also written, but dulled in a black ink. Some had been written and then crossed. It was all there. For a moment, it was scary and chilling. He had been watched and monitored, with every word recorded and every action observed. Angels diligently and tirelessly transcribing all – words, actions and intentions. And here it was, presented without error and without objection. Every word, every deed and every event. Accurate, complete, undeniable. His life's exposé and obituary combined. Signed and sealed with no amendment possible and none required. A definitive statement of history and a compelling narrative of fact.

Certain events were shouting loudly; good deeds were boasting. The time he removed a large, sharp piece of glass from the pavement, saving unaware pedestrians. Selflessly, sincerely and purely. Such a simple act but so high in rank. Unnoticed but totally accepted and recognised. Yes, he remembered what he had done and why he had done it. The small and the regular amount he gave to educate an orphan was also announcing itself and showering him with huge blessings. The supplication he made on his prayer mat, when his child had been buried, tears of anguish and despair falling onto the floor – sincere, pure and full of devotion to the one who took his life. Begging for forgiveness. This deed outshining the others. A beacon of patience and penitence, declaring its glory and greatness.

He held his book in his right hand. Then he glanced to his left. In the distance his fellow passenger was also receiving a book, but in his left hand. When he focused on him the sweet smell of roses, faded to be replaced by a rancid, pungent odour. All who looked and focused at this soul could smell this. Angels and other souls had turned their backs to him. He was being shunned at the time that mattered. His left hand was compelled to take his book which was large and heavy and intimidating. But he had to carry it. It was an immense burden. The Angel presenting it had a dark and gloomy expression. His soul was forlorn and dejected. Pitiful and petrified. Completely powerless. It was not a pleasant sight. He turned away and once again absorbed the warmth and benevolence around him. The book in his hand was light and easy to carry. It beautified him. A divine decoration, a tribute of triumph and an accolade of accomplishment.

He was now allowed to be with his friends and relatives and his son. Time to catch up, but where he did not feel time. His soul then became slightly chilled and he looked worried. "Don't worry Abu," said his son, "it's just your connection with the other world. The false world. This is the real one."

"What's happening?" he asked.

"Your body in the other world is being recovered and prepared for burial." Answered his grandmother. "This is the real world now. This is reality."

Then a sense of peace and tranquillity again. Of warmth and comfort. "People are praying for you," she said. "My son is praying for you, and your children are praying for you."

He looked around and saw beautiful trays of decorated silver coming toward him. Silver goblets full to the brim with sweet tasting juices. Incredibly refreshing. Carried by Angels. His relatives and himself drunk and feasted and were even more rejuvenated. All happily chatting and enjoying. Rose petals like snowflakes falling beautifully around them. Delicate and fragrant. All were visibly touched with his arrival and beaming with happiness. "Your small daughters du'a has been accepted," said his grandmother. "May Allah bless her innocent and sweet heart."

"Ameen," said everyone in unison.

"Ameen," said the good man. He looked down and saw through the mist an image of his little daughter on the prayer mat. Not really understanding what had happened but praying sweetly and innocently, a pure supplication straight from the heart. The height of innocence.

"O Allah, look after my father. Mummy told me he is with you and will not come back as his plane crashed. I miss him and love him. Please tell him as he can't hear me. And stop mummy crying. And also my brother has taken my pencil case and hidden it. Please make him give it back and tell him off as I wanted to colour a picture for my father. Ameen."

The rose petals were thinning and eventually vanished, replaced with a light sprinkle of scented water. It smelled like musk and evaporated as soon as it touched them. Refreshing and sweet, comforting and light. Tremendous tranquillity. All basking in enjoyment.

"It's time daddy," said his son. For him, it was all natural, nothing out of the ordinary. This was real, all else was false and illogical. The world he was born in for a few days - just a dream and irrelevant.

The good man then proceeded to hug all his relatives and different Angels appeared to accompany him back to the earth. Not the same earth but a superimposed one. A dimensional shift in time and space. However, it was real enough. They travelled without speed but almost instantly reached the earth. And there was his body, ready to receive him again. But it wasn't his earthly grave, in his illogical and dream existence before. This was real and it all made sense. Natural and desirable, logical and truthful, correct and proper.

He saw his coffin nearby. There were rows of his friends and family gathered behind him. The funeral prayer had started. He felt a surge of bliss and enormous delight. Then supplications and more peace. He could see all those who had turned out to bid their farewells. He knew they couldn't hear him and knew there was no use in trying to communicate. But he could hear them, loud and clear. They were behind a barrier and would not be able to cross it – not yet anyway. The Priest was conducting the proceedings, and strangely looking at him in his coffin and him in his new existence. The Priest had said to him that their bond would reach beyond this life and now he understood. The good man said *salaam* and the Priest replied. Others present at the funeral were oblivious. His deceased relatives were also watching from above. Far but close. They were happy for him and did not wish him to be unsettled or lonely. However, it was his time and he had to experience it, as they had experienced the joys and ecstasies.

There were also others present. He did not recognise all of them although one or two looked familiar. They were associated with the Priest and came out of love and acknowledgement.

His body was badly burned with damaged limbs patched together. Bones were broken, organs destroyed beyond repair. Skin mottled and many pieces missing with other areas discoloured and ruined because of the sea. Luckily it was relatively shallow and much of the plane and many passengers were recovered. His face though whilst battered and bruised was mostly intact. An expression of peacefulness and sleep, despite the damage. He was shrouded with simple white sheets and perfumed with saffron. And there was a card, coloured by his daughter, resting on his shroud. It had some large gates drawn on it. And there were words at the bottom. 'To Daddy. The gates of paradise are open for you'.

These two Angels now backed away. He looked around. There was a vastness, an expanse. Many people around and many Angels observing. There were also other humans burying their loved ones. He was being buried as well. He saw all his relatives gathered around. Sad. Some were chanting religious verses, and others were quiet. This was not meant to happen, it was not his time, it was too early. His brothers watching painfully. His ageing and distraught father completely broken. He had seen too many funerals and this was not one he had planned to attend. The good man was sad for them, but they did not fully understand. They could never appreciate.

The soil was being filled over his body. With every shovel, a resting and a deep relief. The good man was at peace. And then the final prayer led by the Priest. All raised their hands and supplicated. Waiting tears now released. Pain and torment bare and vocal. And for the good man, with every syllable from the Priest's melodious voice, a relief and a serenity.

Tranquillity and comfort, lightness and happiness filled the good man's soul. His body was now ready to receive him. Not his earthly body, but his new one. Intact and perfect in his new abode. His soul was drawn towards it, an irresistible union.

His feet entered through the neck and lightly and with tremendous ease he became one once again with his body and with a refreshing taste in his mouth. It was the same but different. Like for like, but built for the new dimension.

Not even in a normal grave, but more like an open and spacious garden and field. Warm, inviting, peaceful, not too bright and not too dull. The perfect temperature. There were others but he paid them no heed. Relaxed and comfortable.

He watched as his relatives walked away to continue with their fragile and temporary lives. Their worldly visas still valid for a short time but each would eventually end. His only son was the last to leave. Looking with sadness and with despair at his father's final resting place. His faint existence was now barren and lonely. This was the son with whom the Priest had played badminton a few years before. His father was meant to have died of a heart attack. From that he was saved but from the plane he was not. The son's future appeared to have been ripped away. He was overpowered with hopelessness and despair, misery and depression. Exhaustion could not compete with the emptiness of his soul. For everyone, growing old is compulsory, but growing up is optional. And he had little time now to grow up.

He was now forced to mature many years in as many days. A family to become a head of. A supporting father now no longer able to support. Taken for granted and now taken away forever. And in all this, the Priest's invisible and guiding hand.

# 6.   The Pilgrim

It was the middle of the night.  The student was tired and
hungry and the darkness hot and humid.  But as he struggled
walking in these high temperatures, drained and weary, he
began to see his prize right in front of him.  One vertical side of
this mystical edifice suddenly came into view, and then the
remainder slowly revealed itself as he walked closer towards it.
An epic drama was about to unfold.  Wonderful.  Breathtaking.
Truly amazing.  Beyond words and beyond description.
Inspiring, ... and ... a little scary.  A huge, cubic structure,
towering above those who were present and absent.
Thousands were circumnavigating this spiritual monument in
an endless stream of unordered and ordered groups;  revolving
continuously in chaotic circles.  An image of dynamism,
movement and continuity.  Wheels within wheels and spirals
within circles.  Illuminated by powerful lights, but it's own
brilliance glowing far brighter and more potent for those who
could see.

Veiled in humility as bricks and mortar.  Draped in a rich,
dark cloth, hugging and displaying its might and splendour.
Fitting its strict straight lines firmly and impressively whilst
defining it's immortalized, cubic shape.  An enduring work of
spiritual engineering.  An undying masterpiece of inter-
dimensional art immersed in mystical mastery.  Championing a
rich, spiritual heritage.  It's central position in the creation
announced, defined and established.  Unchallengeable,
undefeatable and undeniable.  The true centre of worship and
of all that is sacred and holy.  Impressive, blessed and above

worldly comprehension. Concealed from all except those with special hearts. Present in the physical world and continuously shining in the spiritual world. Dominating the universe and defining its eternal glory. Saying nothing but explaining everything. Offering all a chance but giving only to the receptive.

The young student was in tears whilst walking robotically towards it. Like a comatosed patient, gliding with the crowd on his spiritual escalator in the direction of this hypnotic and commanding monolith. A spiritual sculpture and architectural masterpiece. Many people would look at this incredible beacon, but very few would actually see it and out of those who see, even fewer benefit. For the pure, its tranquil guidance pierces through the bedlam of confusion, providing peace in chaotic hearts; focus, direction and clarity in the whirlpool of life. Present in all dimensions but visible in only some. A divine lifeline in a frantic and indifferent planet, with the less fortunate suffocating in their miserable mediocrity.

A brave new world with such unknown beauty and power. It is not what one looks at, but what one sees that counts. It's not what one learns but what one enacts that makes a difference. It's great existence, in solitude, hidden from the world but ever present for the benefit of those who can recognise. Serving a secret purpose for the glory of creation and its infinite diversity. Bringing meaning, beauty and sanity to the void. Transporting from darkness into light for the select few. Only humble hearts can reach out and connect and only patient, peaceful hearts can receive.

And then the circumnavigation. This was a calling for harmony and purification. A path to sanity and guidance. A road leading to all that is good. A circular cleansing and a purging of past mistakes and errors. The deletion of rotten deeds and ideas. A new beginning for those who wish it and no change for those who don't. A secured future for the one who beseeches with sincerity and a fake future for the one who begs with falsity. One gets what one comes for and leaves with what one gets. Erasing a difficult past and paving the future with hope.

The student was prepared for this. He hadn't just arrived, but had been summoned. It was his right, his necessity and his destiny. So he circled the blessed structure, again and again and again. Seven times anticlockwise in harmony with all that is good. Then he walked between two small hills in memory of a great saint and the miracles associated therein. Gaining with every step and with every breath and with every heartbeat. Spirituality upon spirituality, blessing upon blessing, light upon light.

After some hours he completed his requisites and then collapsed in a heap of tears and joy. Physically and mentally exhausted but spiritually elated with energy for the final supplication. A connection of the heart, hands and soul; a pleading and beseeching; a begging and a design for the future; the boldness of a youthful need. This was not just his personal journey, one for his individual future, it was also for all those he was destined to help and all those he was destined to defeat. A few hours of effort and worship, permeating and fortifying his entire future. This blessed cube, a spiritual lens, seeking the yearning hearts to cleanse and then fill to the brim with purity and goodness.

The duties had all been completed and the efforts had been accepted. However, for the young student this was the first step on his long journey. It had only just begun and now he realised. An awakening in a confused and dying world. Full of duty, responsibility and very little hope... but incredible spiritual wonder. Clothed in his death shroud. Meek and yearning as he supplicated and pondered his future. His death and then his life and then his death again.

Much had been made clear to him. Much he had to do and he was eager to start. But to start would mean leaving this sacred and blessed place. He would need to take it with him, somehow. So he supplicated for what he needed. He begged, he beseeched and he begged again, irresistibly. He was desperate and so his submissiveness was total. Every atom of his being so engaged and so determined. This greatly pleased the Creator and He wanted to reward him with what he had asked for. With difficulty and trouble, with strife and hardship, with defeat and victory. To be banished into a sober reality where there was no room for pretence.

People come to this mystical place and all they see is a large, black cube. Others see a wonder of mystery and magic but they cannot comprehend. They mentally marvel and spiritually swoon. Very few arrive and then leave after seeing everything they need to. Enrichment and fulfilment. An eternal connection, signed, sealed and soon to be delivered.

Finally the time had come. Time to leave. What sad, sad decisions we have to make. They maybe the saddest ones, but they are indeed the right ones. So with great trepidation he left, although he would never leave. His soul resonating with a new connection and elevated to a new plane of his reality.

# 7.   The Holiday House

The whole family were excited. A lovely villa in Morocco with a swimming pool. Warm, new and exotic. Leaving behind the cold, wintery UK. As it was the season of frost and cold, it would be correct to apply unnecessary, exaggerated adjectives for a major topic of complaint and unnecessary discussion. Thus a better description of Winter would be bleak, dark, rainy, and miserable.

An uneventful journey from the house to the airport. Usual queues at check in and security, then the flight in the twin-engined plane and finally the landing in the strange, hot, humid country. It felt different and it looked different as they were herded from corridor to counter to hall and eventually out of the airport.

The taxi journey to the holiday villa was a good 45 minutes but the driver knew the way. He appeared mature and sensible rather than young and flash. Lethargic afternoon weather and a nice, safe and slow driver. And then they saw it over the hill in the road. It was lovely. There were a few villas, mostly incomplete but this one looked finished, contrasting with the surrounding land which looked derelict and dilapidated. The views were also impressive as the land was higher than its surroundings and most of the district could be seen. Houses sitting idly in the afternoon sun with a slight haze in the air. Lovely patches of trees between the shining roads which hugged the contours of the gentle hills. A lazy landscape

They unloaded the luggage and as the father paid the taxi driver, the children just ran into the villa dragging their mother with them. Tiredness just not registering as it was excitement after excitement, adventure after adventure.

The three children were arguing about which rooms they would be taking. The parents just relieved that they were more or less on schedule. All felt relaxed and excited in the late afternoon heat.

Eventually, they had all chosen their rooms (or rather the parents had convinced them that they had chosen their rooms) and all had settled in the kitchen to feast on some local delicacies. These had been pre-ordered by the owner, keen to look after his guests, at least at the beginning of their stay. Large spicy fish, triangular *naan*, meat balls in curry and fizzy drinks. For the children an adventure and for the parents a change of scene rather than a break.

The sun had set and it was now night time. Children playing surprisingly happily in their rooms and more surprisingly playing together. No fighting or arguing. Idyllic.

As it got later into the night and the family were preparing to change and sleep, there appeared to be someone at the door. It was a loud and aggressive banging. Not the normal gentle knocking of a polite person but someone angry and in haste and with something urgent to say. The wife looked at the husband, slightly worried. But this was a man's regime and the husband went into 'man mode', marching towards the door with the intention of challenging this rude behaviour. It did not matter what language this visitor could or could not speak, he would be confronted and told off in a manner that he would understand.

The children had gathered around the mum and they looked worried because the mother looked worried. The young son though followed his father. There was a small frosted window in the door but not one to see out of easily. Certainly no outline of any person outside. The father grabbed the door handle and aggressively opened the door, ready for confrontation. And there was....nothing. No-one. Not a sausage. The little boy peered around the fathers legs and said, "Huh! There is no-one." The father then stepped outside into the dark, warm chill and looked around, not venturing too far but still in 'man-mode'. Still no-one. His son now at his heels. Strange. "Local children pranking," said the father to his family. "There cannot be any other explanation. Either they were hiding or had run off into the darkness. They must know this area well to be out at this time with so little light."

Time to put the excited kids to bed. As long as they were in their rooms it was fine if they were playing and chatting. They were all changed, fed, watered with plates empty, ready to enter their next stage of the night – chat and play and then hopefully drop off to sleep. This was then the time for the parents to have their quiet cup of tea, watching the satellite TV channels. Three kids, split into two rooms with interconnecting doors. The two elder girls together and the youngest boy on his own.

Then it happened. A loud bang and then instant darkness throughout the house. All the electricity suddenly disconnected. The TV flickered as its image disappeared leaving a faint glow across the whole of the flat screen. There were no lights outside and it was pitch black inside. Screams came from the girls' room and then a thud.

"Don't try and move around in the dark," shouted the father has he hastily got out of bed and fumbled for and then grabbed his mobile. "Put your mobiles on" he shouted. (Finally a useful use for this expensive toy.)

He put his mobile on and the lit screen was enough to light his way. With his arms stretched out in front of him he headed to where the door was. "I'm coming," he said reassuringly, "it's only the fuse." He was met in the hallway by his children who all had managed to switch their torches on. The LEDs shining whitely, brightly and coldly. An eerie scene with long, new shadows moving around. The father then selected his phone options and managed to find the torch and switched his on as well.

"Go and keep your mother company," he said to them all as he thought of how he was going to find the fuse box. The kids all scuttled into the master bedroom, the mother grateful for the company. Back in 'man mode' (the DIY version), he went off in search of the elusive, foreign fuse box. No idea where it was, what it looked like or what sort of design it would be. It seems like a trip, which hopefully meant that it could be easily switched back on.

All the obvious places searched and no luck. Time to get help from the owner. Luckily he had stored his number in his phone. After a short conversation, he ventured outside. And there it was, the fuse box in the most unexpected place, on the outside wall at the back behind an obstinate bush. He managed to open it and it seemed somewhat familiar with modern trip switches. The master switch was off, while all the others – including the trip was in the on position. Strange. He switched on the master and heard shrieks of happiness as the lights went on in the house. He returned triumphant. 'Man mode' had been successful.

After that excitement, an uneventful night. All slept, all woke, all had breakfast, all went out sightseeing and all came back. A second night now loomed with the previous night's events forgotten.

Another ordered meal, this time more closer to home, pizza, chips and drinks. All partook in the mini feast devouring every spicy crumb.

While eating, a strange noise from the basement. They knew there was a basement as a sign on the door stated as such although none had yet investigated it. The door was a simple one, different to all the normal room-doors, looking old, plain and dull. It preferred to go unnoticed. An old entrance to an irrelevant place. Another noise, this time louder. It sounded as if there was someone down there. It was a loud shuffling as if heavy furniture was being moved and dropped. "It's probably outside," said the father wishing to finish his slice rather than venture downstairs. Then a noise which could not be mistaken. A scream from the basement and then a loud, urgent banging on the basement door – from the other side. All jumped. The mother let out a shriek. All went quiet... all looked scared... all felt a chill. All were looking at the basement door. Man-mode on hold.

The father's slice had frozen in mid-air in-between the plate and his mouth, bending slightly under the weight of the cheese and spicy chicken. His mouth also stopped chewing and his face had turned towards the cellar door along with everyone else's. 'Why does it have to be the cellar door?' he asked himself.

The father moved his chair back and slowly re-started chewing his mouthful while he carefully placed his slice onto his plate. 'Whatever happens, I am going to finish that slice,' he thought. He checked his phone and put on the torch light. Now in automatic man-mode, he got up and walked towards the cellar his son close behind, but not too close. He ignored pleas from his mum to come and stay with her. The girls stayed with their mum, cuddling up to her, clearly frightened and all breathing fast. He stretched out his hand and turned the handle, looked back at his son ensuring he was far enough back and then armed with his mobile phone torch, menacing face and a maximum release of adrenalin, threw open the door ready for anything. There he saw a wall of darkness. A cold wisp of air smelling damp and stale chilled his nose and throat. He saw the light switch on the wall and pressed it but it did not come on.

'Typical,' he thought, 'just typical. Stupid house!'

He shone his mobile phone torch downstairs only glimpsing the first few concrete stairs.

"Don't go down," screamed his wife. "Are you mad?"

"No," he answered, not looking back and he stepped onto the first concrete stair shining his torch down. This was a matter of his families safety and of him showing his children how not to be afraid. He can't back down now. So he slowly went down the stairs, his useless, gimmicky torch lighting up hardly anything. As it is with mobiles – toys with very few useful applications. Essentially a mobile chit-chat device and games machine to pass the time. Not essential to living but no-one can live without it.

Nothing. Absolutely nothing. Only a few empty chairs laid out as if people had just been sitting having a chin-wag and had literally just left. The cellar was quite large though. Lots of dark corners. He had a quick look around and then went back up the stairs only to meet his son with his mobile torch on, coming slowly down the stairs.

"There is nothing here." He said. "It was probably screams and bangs outside."

"But we heard them from here," said his son. He was in his own mini 'man mode' as he had just turned ten and knew he must follow his father.

"But as you can see. Nothing here."

"Could it have been a *Jinn*?" asked his son.

"We don't talk about that." Replied his father. "Especially at this time."

They left the cellar stairs and the father closed the door. It wasn't easy, but eventually they all slept and got up in the morning. No-one really had a comfortable night and all woke up tired. All the lights had been left on, all doors ajar and all phones charged and at the ready.

They made the best of the day, travelling, sightseeing, eating. A change of scene welcome from the mundane routine of life and being away from the villa which had been mostly forgotten. As the day passed and sunset approached, however, the parents began thinking more and more about it. The children had all but forgotten the previous night's events as they were distracted for the whole day. New environment, new weather, new surroundings, new activities.

But now the time had come. The return. The Villa appeared at the end of the road in the darkness. The headlights of the taxi lit up the front door as the car came to a halt. It looked different and eerie. Cold and unwelcoming. The family piled out of the car and the children rushed to the front door with all their gifts and bags from the day being dragged and carried and kicked along the ground. The mother trying to control them but was not heard in the excitement while the father paid the taxi driver. The mother opened the door and the children raced in as if a starter gun had gone off. Switching on the lights whilst running and heading at full speed to their rooms. The humdrum drowning out her words of 'quietly,' 'carefully', 'get changed into your night clothes' etc. etc.

It took over an hour to settle everyone down until the couple were able to sit down and enjoy a cup of tea. They had eaten out already so no official family dinner required. Kids were quietly chatting and playing in their bedrooms upstairs and husband and wife were in the main bedroom downstairs next to the kitchen.

The parents were just relaxing watching a documentary on climate change when suddenly they heard a scream and footsteps running towards their room. They recognised the scream – it was their eldest daughter. Their two girls then ran into their parent's room and flung themselves into their arms.

"We saw it!" one of them shouted. "We saw it!"

"What, what?" asked their mum repeatedly.

"In the cellar, we saw it!"

"What...what?"

The father checked on his son who was fast asleep and then came back to fathom what was going on. On the way back he saw the cellar door wide open and a faint light illuminating part of the floor, the walls and the door.

"You've been in the cellar?" he asked quickly.

The eldest girl nodded in guilt and with tears in her eyes, sniffing and hyperventilating. "We saw it." She kept repeating. "It was a dead body and it moved."

"Covered in white sheets," said the youngest daughter. "It moved."

The parents both looked at each other, horrified. "It was just a bad dream," said the mother trying to comfort them.

"The cellar door is wide open," said the father. "I believe them." I must go and have a look."

"No!" his wife screamed. "Let's just leave, let's go from here."

"Don't be silly, it might just be a trick of the light, let me see."

Even though his wife had grabbed his arm, he wriggled free and was determined to go and have a look. He had to. Not 'man-mode' any more, now up a grade to 'soldier mode'. His wife was in 'horror film, scared, heroine, victim, panic mode'.

He peered through the cellar door, only to hear his wife come to the front of her bedroom door, girls clinging to her. He took a deep breath and then his first shaky step. He fumbled for his phone and put the torch light on, even though the cellar light was now on. He took a second, less shaky step and then squatted down to look around. He peered with his full focus and concentration. And he saw....nothing. No weird dead body. No shrouded person. No ghost. 'Soldier mode' now downgraded to 'man-mode'. He walked down a few more steps and kept looking around. Just those few empty chairs. It looked exactly the same and smelled exactly the same. Weird and uncomfortable, damp and chilly.

After a minute or so, he called his wife and daughters to the cellar door. Surprisingly, they all slowly came. With their father now deep within the cellar, it seemed a little safer. However, they would not go past the door. Observing from the top with their mother there for protection was enough.

They had dared each other to go down into the cellar. The elder one manipulating the younger one. They were both eager and very quietly did the deed. Half-way down though they stopped when they saw a shrouded figure of a person lying on the floor. Definitely an outline of a body under a few white sheets. That was upsetting enough. And just when they were about to turn and run as fast as they could up the stairs, the face turned, creasing the sheets and looked directly towards them. Auto scream and panic mode took over and they both struggled past each other and raced to their parent's room.

They eventually went to their rooms and with great difficulty fell asleep. Semi-convinced it was a trick of the light. They felt a little safer now a large trunk had been placed against the cellar door. "No-one can get out of there now, said their father, "not even a dead person." How they didn't laugh.

The next day was uneventful. This country looked the same as the first day and they returned a little later than normal.

"I'm just going to the kitchen to get some more biscuits," said the mum as she left her husband to watch the drama type film that was showing. She didn't bother with her dressing gown as the kitchen was just opposite the bedroom and the children were unlikely to come downstairs. In any case it would take too long and the night was warm. She hurried into the kitchen and opened the end cupboard where the biscuits had been sort of hidden. She picked up the packet and turned to go back to the bedroom. She stopped suddenly and jumped. Her husband was standing in the doorway of the kitchen smiling.

"You scared me," she said giggling.

"Sorry," he replied. "Just thought it was a good idea to show you something in another room. Just forgot all about it until now."

"What is it?" she asked.

"It's just towards the back in the spare bedroom. It's quite amusing."

"Ok," she said, a bit disappointed at her tea and biscuits being delayed but followed her husband towards the back of the house. It was strange though how his hair seemed to have lost a bit of its greyness and was quite tidy. This was more than likely to have been as the result of the dimmed lights so she didn't pay it much attention. She has also noticed his rather plain, clean and crisp skin colour. A little paler than normal but also dismissed it.

Anyway, they both scurried to the back room and went in, the wife first. A strange, cold, white, dim light was already on and contrasted the room walls against its contents. A few cupboards, boxes and shelves. It seemed like a spare room that had never been used. Cobwebs now appeared in the corners of the room as her eyes became used to the light.

"What do you want to show me?" she asked, as she looked around. There appeared to be nothing of any consequence. Her husband closed the door gently behind her.

She turned to face him slightly confused but also still curious and a little excited. His face had changed, now looking quite serious and entirely blank. An odd expression with strange, lifeless eyes.

It happened suddenly and without warning. His hand grabbed her throat and squeezed. It was so tight and so swift that she could not breathe or scream. The perfectly placed hold was choking her. Her other hands grappled his to try and move it off. But the grip was strong and the arm immovable. Her legs started giving way. His face was totally expressionless. Time slowed down as her brain processed everything a top speed. His eyes cold and detached from reality. Completely dispassionate. Her legs now began to collapse but she was still held up by his powerful arm. Her reflexes caused her legs to try and support her weight as she frantically kicked the ground with her bare feet and still helplessly tried to move his arm. It was hopeless and it was terrifying. She had been turned all around now and her back was to the door. She was being pressed against it as her lungs were now desperate for air. Her head was becoming light and her face was turning blue as her body was starved of oxygen. Her brain had also started to react to the lack of oxygen. Nothing was working. Her throat was being squeezed tighter and his hand seemed to be enormous. Double its normal size and many times its normal strength wrapped completely around her throat. Her arms now collapsed, just twitching and her legs slowly stopped working as she began to lose consciousness.

There was then a knock on the door and her husband suddenly released her. She fell as an uncontrolled heap onto the floor gasping and breathing frantically. No breath to scream let alone speak or even groan.

"What's happening?" shouted her husband as he tried to open the door from outside the room. It was stuck and after a couple of times trying to push it, he shouldered it. It opened abruptly, smacking into her head. But she was too weak and too dazed to realise. Her lungs were painfully working

73

overtime, catching up. Her head was extremely heavy as she half-opened her eyes. She looked up at the door which was now pressed against her shoulder only to see, with blurred vision, her husband looking in. He was trying to push the door open and squeeze through the gap into the room. She looked the other way towards the man who had just been strangling her. There was no-one there. Her husband now with his full body pushed opened the door as quickly as he could, sliding her around as she lay helpless on the dusty laminate floor. He rushed in with a look of utter shock on his face when he saw her bent down and blue in the face to pick her up. She was confused as he had just tried to kill her but he was now outside the room? She was baffled and helpless and did not understand as she fainted with these thoughts all muddled in her weak, throbbing head.

Once all had been explained, and understood and he had ensured his wife was okay, the father quickly woke up the children and bought them all into his room. His wife had regained consciousness and he had placed her on their bed. She was sitting with a glass of water and an aspirin. He searched the house thoroughly to find this 'person' who had impersonated him, but elected not to go into the cellar. He then urgently phoned the Priest.

That night, all slept in one room with the lights on all over house, but with the continuous inner fear of another power cut. TV on and mobile torches at the ready. The kids slowly fell asleep scattered around the parent's bed, but the parents stayed awake till dawn. The father sat in the 'comfy chair' which wasn't really very comfortable while the wife sat on the bed

74

with the children around her. She had refused her husband from calling a doctor and just wanted to leave immediately but she was too scared to leave and too scared to stay. There were strange noises outside in the dark surrounding. She was still in a state of shock. With every noise they both jumped and became scared. Only once the new light of day began to illuminate the room and gradually got brighter did the husband finally fall asleep for a short time, and then eventually his wife. An uncomfortable and difficult night with confusing and scary dreams.

The parents were both deeply disturbed. Totally confused as to what had happened. They had phoned the Spirit Priest and he had advised them exactly what they had to do. He told them to start packing and to leave after sunrise and that they would be safe until then. However, they should all stay together in the same room as much as possible, always go in pairs and keep all the lights on. He assured them that they had backing and support and they would be safe for the next few hours. The Priest, was for the time being, blocking this powerful demon from attempting anything. The Priest also knew that this was a dangerous situation and they kept in touch on the phone. Better they stayed together and move out in daylight than leave immediately as there was more danger outside. This had been an unprecedented attack. An evil and powerful beast from another world had shown his authority and might.

So they started packing and were ready to move out just after sunrise. It was then the husband started to phone all the local hotels and eventually found one. The day was spent moving, settling in and resting rather than sightseeing. Not a holiday but a very painful experience, more like a hell-a-day. One to be forgotten but one which would be remembered. The wife would need counselling by the Priest for a few years and the demon would also need to be dealt with. A very unfortunate situation indeed. Few people could have survived and even fewer could have dealt with this incident. Intense, shocking and terrifyingly real.

They endured, not because of their inner strength or their bravery. No. They survived because of the hidden help they received. Help which is only apparent to a few but powerful and essential nevertheless. There were only a handful of people who had the position and permission to deal with this. Luckily for them the Spirit Priest was one of these rare and hidden gems. He has been and is such men. Undiscovered, unknown, unpretentious. Bringing some sort of order to a world of terror and chaos.

# 8. *Daddy*

"When is he coming?" she asked again for the twentieth time.

The little girl was lying in her hospital bed staring at the door. Her mum was sitting by her side in a chair reading a book.

"Hmmm", said her mother in automatic mode, meaning 'soon'. She was absorbed in her novel.

The room was warm and a little stuffy but somewhat ventilated with irregular wisps of warm, wafting air. It was a cold, late afternoon. A weak, wintery sun low down in the horizon casting some long shadows in this private room. The time of day when the body slows down and the mind wants to relax a bit. One's natural siesta slowly overcoming and overpowering the body and the mind. The little girl had throat cancer. She was finding it difficult to swallow and had given up solids for some weeks now. She was wasting away as the drips and fluids feeding her veins were not substantial enough to sustain her feeble existence. A slow and steady starvation. Surgeons could not operate effectively without seriously injuring or even killing her. They had given up. No Doctor or surgeon in the world could save her.

For the little girl though, it was a very simple equation. She wanted to see her daddy who had promised to come back from his car showroom to see her. Her eyes transfixed, staring at the door. Her throat pain was constant, occasionally dulled with morphine but she had been seriously weakened. Her Daddy always made her feel better and special. He was her best medicine.

The parents had sought assistance from the Priest when she had been diagnosed, but he looked upset. He worked to minimise her pain and maximise the time and effort her parents spent with her. He had advised them that medical science was going to struggle to cure her and they may have to prepare for the worst. There are some things that are destined and decided and cannot be changed. They are written, sealed and done.

It had been only two years ago when she had fallen onto the ground littered with building material in her garden. A small piece of lead flashing had pierced her throat. The parents had taken her to see a doctor who had removed what he thought was all the contamination, but there was a tiny scrape that evaded detection and had found a resting place deep within. Cells were damaged and their chromosomes affected. They then began splitting and generating uncontrollably. Then it was too late and the lump in the throat would eventually spread and kill her. Now she was nine but would not live to double figures.

It was a difficult two years as all treatments failed and a slow, creeping starvation was the inevitable end. A petite, weak body already, becoming more fragile and feeble as each day passed. Her body failing. Her life slowly dissipating. Her strength and being both evaporating.

It was a tragedy pure and simple. The sordid and untouchable dark side of life. An obvious truth. One to be avoided but cannot be avoided. Firmly fixed in her destiny. An ultimate sacrifice and a n unimaginable position to be in. But they were in it, right at the deep end and there was no-one who could help. The world's top experts quietly powerless. Shamefully hiding their expertise but bare for all to see. All resigned to the inevitable end of an innocent young life, who had not known life and could not imagine death.

It was the desire for her father that kept her strong. He was her hero. A sincere love and an innocent thirst, quenched by her fathers affection. He was her life and he was her cure.

Her eyes were still looking towards the door of her room, waiting for her father to open it, smile and greet her in his normal, cheerful way. He made her forget the discomfort and pain. He bravely hid his vast pain and grief, fiercely fighting back each tear. His little princess must never realise as her happiness would extend her life and her final months must be as happy as possible. He was convinced and so cried quietly and privately whenever he could. In the car, in the bathroom and under the covers of his bed. His life was ending as hers was ending, but his sense of duty and deep affection kept him going. He was dead in his existence. Always on the edge of a breakdown but somehow holding himself together. His heart ached when his daughter could not eat at mealtimes. He was her protector and father and guardian and her daddy, but was totally and utterly powerless. A deep, powerful throbbing pain that hurt a lot. How does one cope in this situation? Because one has to.

The hospital was relatively new but looked well used. The large door to her room was scratched, battered and bruised. It's wood polish whilst trying to hide the mechanical damage, glistened in the afternoon sun as it pierced the gaps through the window blinds.

This is not how life is meant to pan out. It was meant to be heavenly and it had turned out to be the opposite. But it must be faced and this pathetic fight must continue. The battle must be fought even if there was defeat in sight as some journeys cannot be lenghtened and cannot be avoided. It must progress or it will be worse. How weak and fragile we actually are although we think of ourselves as immortal and always in control. The devastation was huge and his derelict heart helpless and in ruins. Angry and upset, in a deep and private turmoil. He was emotionally distraught and spiritually destitute.

Her Daddy was held up in his place of work. Trying to persuade customers to buy his cars, while his daughter was dying. All so that he could look after his family, pay his insensitive bills and his emotionless creditors. He was living a detached and surreal existence while his precious princess gradually ebbed into the next world.

"He's still not here mummy," she cried, weakly. "He promised and I want to see him."

Her mother turned the page of her book and looked up at her daughter. She put the book down and then stroked her daughters head, trying to comfort her. "Don't worry, he's on his way," she tried to explain. "He's coming."

"No, he promised," she cried, as tears of sadness and frustration oozed out of her weary eyes. She was too weak to cry intensely. Just a weak and quiet sobbing. Her tears struggled to emerge from her weakened body while her sobbing continued. "I miss him and I can't help it," she lamented.

The loneliness. The silent screams. The wailing soul. No one to turn to and no one to help. Nothing to look forward to except the inevitable. Life is a prison of pain and torment. An invisible blaze in which we burn.

Her mother tried her best to comfort her, but all she could hope for was for her to fall asleep. Here was their dichotomy. They were in financial trouble so her father had to work. He did make it to the hospital every evening, but sometimes was late depending upon customers. He daren't close early as he needed the business. Anyway, his wife had been texting him so he had begun the routine to close his business. His little princess was unusually upset and he had to go and see her.

She had paused in her crying now and was staring at the door. Her mother hoped now she would drift into sleep as she had a difficult and interrupted rest the night before. The TV was normally off as her daughter could not take too much noise and the flickering light upset her weakened eyes. Anyway, she was quiet now and her father was on his way. He would take around an hour or so to arrive. Soon she would be happy and a little rejuvenated when she saw him. Her mother went back to her novel. It served as a distraction and welcome occupation of time. She drifted into her false reality and glanced at her daughter every now and again. She saw she was quiet and looking at the door, waiting.

Then the time finally came. He arrived. Her father. He walked in full of life and energy and a big smile on his face. Doing well to hide his pain and upset. Terribly tired. He saw his daughter looking half-asleep and staring straight at him with her half-open eyes, and his smile got even broader and his tiredness disappeared. He walked straight to his little princess and his wife closed her novel to greet him. However, his daughter did not smile or move or say anything. She was still. Her delicate and blameless body cool. She had stopped breathing some time ago and her heart would never beat again. Her motionless eyes still fixed on the door, waiting.

# 9.   A Spiritual Landscape

The student had returned to the Priest's office and was sitting in his presence. Upset, wanting, yearning. It had been two whole years since he had been able to sit with the Spirit Priest in this manner. In that time he had been through turmoil after turmoil; trouble, toil and torture. A number of close family had passed away, plus he had experienced some deeply personal and traumatic events. A rollercoaster of trials and tribulations; at times wishing he had been dead. He felt as if he had been taken to death's door and had pushed it open, staring into the abyss. Now his pride and arrogance completely anesthetised. Intoxicated by his spiritual awareness and numbed by events. He had been blunted by life's ferocity and now he was dead; dead and ready. A clear, blank canvass, ready for the Priest's spiritual artistry.

He was sitting in-front of the Priest. Quiet, humble; not eager to speak or impress – just seeking. Each soul is created differently and each needs a different touch. Precious few have the gift required to undertake such delicate work. Subtle yet gentle, placid but powerful, potent and purposeful. His soul required illumination and enhancement, fortification and authority. This was not what he had in mind. This was not what he expected. What had happened was frighteningly real and desperately difficult at all possible levels. He had tripped and fallen and then had been kicked whilst he was down. Embarrassed, exasperated and humiliated. Drained and exhausted. His youthful energies all but gone. Hopes and aspirations all eliminated and dreams and ambitions all neutralised. Now an empty shell. He was finished and he was ready to start.

The Priest was breathing calmly. He looked at his young student and was pleased. His future could now begin and take shape - and take shape well. Fitting nicely into the global plan. He was ready.

"How are you?" asked the Priest.

"*Alhamdulillah*," replied the young man. Quiet, thoughtful and with no expectations. His reply rich in need and full of meaning but devoid of any pride.

It was a chilly spring morning. Thick, low clouds dulled the sun. A hazy, fluffy ceiling laden with moisture. The Priest's office though was pleasant and warm. They were both enjoying a lovely, sweet, caffeine rich coffee. Not 'decaff', or 'de-coloured' or 'de-flavoured, or 'de-toxed'. Not even 'herbal rich' or 'de' anything. Just a strong, sugary cup of caffeine, milk, instantaneous coffee-bean rich nectar. 'Re-toxing' was required at this time and 'de-toxing' could wait.

The Priest now had an interesting question with a seemingly simple answer. However, it was laden with profundity and rich in consequence. "What does that mean," he asked?

It was not the smartness of the young student that answered the question, not his intelligence nor even his experience. The answer was coloured and determined by the sincerity of his heart.

"Whatever the Almighty wishes, I am happy with," he responded with a sincere and grateful smile. He was unconcerned as to whether the answer was correct. His innermost being was speaking.

The young man had seen more than a person usually is permitted to see and had experienced far more than most are allowed to experience. He had already lived a number of lifetimes but was still in his first. Young in age but old in experience and maturity. On one occasion, he had been mugged in South London. Two people asked him the time and looked innocent and friendly. It had just rained and the night had started in earnest. He was going home after a day at university lectures. It was drizzling and the streets were wet and shiny. Most cars negotiating the roads carefully with lights being reflected everywhere. A damp and dreary scene with tyres splashing patchy puddles and pedestrians rushing around in their own worlds fearing every raindrop. Others showing off their fearlessness, challenging the light rain.

The student was concerned and became prepared for an altercation. However, these muggers were experienced and had done this before. They were fast, powerful and well coordinated. A couple of hardened, fearless street thugs, specially chosen for hunting the streets. As they asked him the time, one produced a gun and dug it deep into his ribs while the other mugger firmly grabbed his arm and took him into a dark side street, flanked closely by his colleague. Ignored by passersby who were busy dodging the raindrops. They forcefully took his jacket off and went through the pockets, finding nothing. They threw it aside. The mugger with the gun then instructed his companion to search his trouser pockets. Still nothing. The student listened to the sounds in the street nearby. Life proceeding as normal, uncaring and unconcerned. The hustle and bustle, immune and indifferent. The rain still gently falling quietly and uncaringly. Still the muggers found nothing. They must continue this ordeal.

He suddenly felt a sharp pain in his lower back as he was punched with full force. He collapsed onto the floor, doubled and on his knees. The mugger with the gun was extremely angry at having got nothing. They both started a heated discussion in their native Russian language. Loud and angry voices trying to whisper. He then he felt his hair grabbed and his head twisted upwards only to see the gun being thrust right into his forehead. Every instinct told him they were going to pull the trigger. He was staring at deaths door and he needed to try and control his destiny. With all his strength he grabbed the gun pointing it away whilst in the same motion, his other hand had formed a firm fist with which he punched the mugger in the groin. It was powerful and accurate. The mugger groaned in pain and collapsed onto the floor, dropping his gun; both his hands on his pain. The student then rolled out of the way but was kicked in his head by the other mugger. He continued to roll out of the way and tried to get up. He was struggling. Another kick, this one missed as he was moving a little too fast. Not good enough though, as he tripped and fell on the slippery ground whilst trying to get up. Now both muggers were on him. They wanted vengeance, especially the one with the throbbing groin.

He was now dragged further into the darkness. A powerful motorcycle drove by and paid no attention. The motorcyclist with pictures of demons on his leathers. So much for Hells

Angels. The punching and kicking continued. Head, back, ribs, groin. A pause. Then it happened. The gun held against the side of his head and the trigger being pulled. Instinctively the student managed to place his finger behind the trigger as both his hands had grabbed the gun. The mugger put his full force and couldn't operate the trigger. The gun being twisted one way then the other. The other mugger tried to drag his hand out of the way, but the student would not budge. He was holding on as his life depended upon it. Then another volley of punches and stamping, but he still would not submit. The muggers groaning as they applied maximum force in their onslaught. Suddenly his wrist went limp. Then a loud bang and a searing pain. They had stamped onto his hand and dislocated his wrist, breaking a number of bones. The gun had gone off as his finger slipped out. They wrestled the smoking gun now free from his floppy hand and casually walked off, merging into the darkness, thinking they had shot him. The busy noise of the street continued as the student lost consciousness, laying in an undignified heap. Blood oozing out of his nose and the light rain gently washing it away.

He had not been shot. Many passers-by, just passed by, making excuses to themselves. No one has any time for humanity in this selfish and greedy world. An old man walking his dog stumbled on this pathetic scene observed by an inhumane society and staged for their indifference. He called an ambulance, doing his best with the zero medical knowledge he had. An unknown hero in the midst of selfishness, impatience and darkened souls.

It took the student several days in hospital to recover sufficiently to be discharged home. Plus months of operations, medicines and physiotherapy. Any other person would have been thankful to have survived. This student was grateful to have been permitted to have gone through this test and to have failed, as you cannot break the broken. He was learning. Verily relief comes with difficulty, indeed, relief comes with difficulty.

The Priest looked deep into the soul of this young man. He smiled, but not with his lips. He smiled with his heart. That was the right answer. That would see him through. That was the lesson to have been learnt and he has learned it well. This was not a translation of '*Alhamdulillah*', it was an understanding of it. A proper understanding. This was the foundation of his future and it was good, strong and what was required.

"Let me ask you about our purpose in life?" the Priest continued. He knew he would get a deep, rich and inspiring answer. He was right.

"The one who asks, knows much more than the one being asked. Much, much more. I am still learning and yearning the answer. I am content with what has happened and with what will happen. I am at the service for those who need. *Alhamdulillah*."

The Priests internal smile grew larger. He was happy and content. The training was going well, but there was still a long, long way to go. Facing death's door would not be enough for this young apprentice. He would have to go through it and then return. This way he would learn and this way he would die before his death. *Alhamdulillah*.

# 10.  A Table, a Quilt and a Candle

It was indeed a revelation.  The parents were sitting opposite the Priest in his small office on one of his surgery days.  They were content and they were smiling.  Spring was trying to make its mark but the morning frosts were fighting it.  A bitter cold blanket was slowly passing across the entire country, saturating it with sub-zero temperatures and freezing everything it could.  This resulted in many unwelcome inevitable conversations about the weather, stating the obvious.

"So," continued the Priest, this time to the father.  "What is your most memorable family experience?"

The father had to pause and think.  He was quite surprised at his wife's answer and was still trying to come to terms with it.  The Priest saw he was thinking and was also struggling to think.  So, he decided to help.

"Let me help," he said helpfully.  "There is a famous chat show host, whom I shall not name.  She was asked this question, and I have to say, she is still one of the most famous and wealthy in her field.  Her answer was extremely surprising.  Her best and most fondest memory was of her in the car with her husband.  It was dark and rainy and she was very uncomfortable.  So her husband suggested that they sing songs.  She reluctantly agreed.  So they sang for the whole journey until they arrived at their destination.  Now bear in mind that she was rich, powerful and famous.  You would have thought her most memorable event was a holiday to an exotic location.  Maybe a large family party.  Even a wedding anniversary.

Possibly the purchase of her favourite mansion. But no - it was a silly little sing song with the one whom she loved. Their voices were not even very good. But that was her most memorable family moment."

The husband and wife were looking at the Priest. They had come to see him for some advice on parenting. They had a young family who were in the waiting room, being looked after by an 'aunty'. The children were taking full advantage of this young aunty who was well out of her comfort zone and appeared to have no authority over them. The three little tornados aged from two till five were well in control and completely ignoring all her appeals and requests. To the children, this aunty was a gift. Opening this and closing that; walking in and out of every room; rearranging peoples shoes; even trying to go into areas where no visitor was allowed. There was an interesting cupboard under the stairs but it looked a bit scary and was ignored as the eldest child commented there was a 'big *babba*' hiding there.

The waiting room was as child proof as possible with all decorative pieces well out of reach. But children are natural, tireless researchers. Brave, fearless and foolish. If it is within reach, these kids would grab it, explore it, feel it, smell it, taste it and then throw it away with no care or attention so they could quickly move onto the next item. The size of the toy did not worry them. As small as a coaster to as large as a fireplace. Even the long, thick velvety curtains were not immune. All three were at one time stroking different parts of the curtain as it had a beautiful soft and fluffy texture. Then when they got bored they tugged, admired the weight, messed up what they could and then quickly forgot them. The world was their playground – or rather this waiting room would do nicely - and its contents were theirs.

It had turned out to be a sunny, pleasant day but still cold. The occasional white cloud decorated the rich blue sky as it drifted past on this enormous canvas, framed by dull rooftops.

Other clients looked on in the room, but they were consumed by their own personal problems so were not too interested. Quiet, tense and concerned. Just being there provided a sense of peace, although they knew their problems were still waiting and ready to pounce on them.

The father was still brainstorming, trying his best to figure out what memories had really stuck out. He also had to be careful, especially after what his wife had said. There was that *biryani* he had eaten a few years ago at their cousins wedding, but maybe that's not the correct thing to say. What about those kebabs from London when he went out with his friends? Wow, they were something to remember. He had even bought some home for his wife, but managed to eat them on the way back as they were that good. No, it needs to be a family thing. Maybe the day he bought his 340 bhp turbo charged family saloon? Possibly, as after all, the family do ride in it don't they? So his thoughts continued along those lines, convinced he would find something accurate, acceptable and family related.

He was warmly dressed in a polar neck, woolly jumper and comfortable loose black trousers, whilst she had a traditional but insulating *kameez*, with a long, black overcoat, decorated with faint silvery designs and a dark scarf to match.

His wife was eyeing him up, waiting eagerly for his comments. Hopefully he might mention an aspect of their marriage. Maybe their honeymoon? One of the presents she had bought him for his birthday? Maybe the day she told him she was expecting? The birth of their first child? The first birthday she had celebrated with him in their marriage? Possibly the day they chose her special diamond friendship ring which he bought her (after much persuasion) and which he chose for her (also after much persuasion). Her thoughts and ideas were interrupted when the Priest spoke.

"So," encouraged the Priest, "any thoughts?

"Yes," replied the husband. "It was the day we chose my wife's friendship ring. It was indeed a very special day."

"That's wonderful," the Priest commented.

The husband was relieved as he saw his wife's overjoyed smile and the Priests praise. 'Job done', he thought as he began to switch his mind off to go back into his micro-sleep.

Then the Priest commented, "But how about a family occasion, with the children, like the one your wife mentioned?"

The husband was disappointed as he was once again challenged. His mind drifted towards the turbo-charged saloon again as this was now a distinct possibility. Even some of the previous food items he had remembered were also viable candidates. His wife's story about the table, quilt and candle was quite a surprising choice, but he couldn't use that one now she had mentioned it.

So his mind continued to think as he struggled to remember so that he could say the right thing. The path of least resistance. Then a brainwave. 'Of course', he thought. 'That was it'. "The photograph on the bridge", he declared proudly. "The one with all the family on holiday, remember?"

His wife was pleased. She was nodding. Yes, she remembered it well now, although had temporarily forgotten it. She smiled as she made the connections to the photograph, where everyone was standing. The old couple who couldn't use the camera but ended up taking a stunning photograph by mistake. All in focus, and all expressions reflecting their personalities; wonderfully framed and everyone looking happy. The time immediately before when an overweight young gentleman slipped and the children all laughed as he rolled around. Then that lovely boat called 'friendship' went under the elegant and small suspension bridge and the children all waving to their counterparts below. The amazing weather, stunning scenery, fresh air...yes, it was a memorable time.

The husband was now relaxed. Rather more relieved than relaxed in fact. That was a lot of thinking for the weekend, when normally his brain was in 'drift' mode, like a yacht, lazily bobbing up and down in the sea, sails lowered and no wind. The occasional, dull splash of water on its hull providing a lethargic backdrop and a weary soundtrack in which to relax and sleep.

"So why choose the table and candle story?" asked the husband. "Surely the bridge picture is better?"

His wife immediately shook her head. "No," she replied. "The children loved it. Under the table with a candle, and the king sized quilt draped over it as walls. They keep asking to do it again. Plus all the stories we told them. They found it weird and wonderful. Their own little house in the room. We have forgotten as adults what we used to wish for as children. The innocent games and harmless fun. No need for expensive technology, only friendship and love and lots of story telling."

The husband just nodded. He still didn't really understand and neither did he wish to very much. It was uncomfortable under that small table. Designed for children rather than adults, and he had to keep his head a little bent. But that's fine, whatever makes everyone happy. "That's really sweet," he commented. Not really overly enthusiastic, but as long as everyone was happy it meant he had said the right thing. The candle had been a fire hazard anyway.

"So," asked the Priest to the wife. "What else have you done for your children?"

The wife now turned to the Priest, eager to update him on recent events. So she explained how she had found all the best websites with useful songs and cartoons and goes through them with the children on their smart TV rather than they getting used to watching meaningless cartoons. Then how she worked with them to produce drawings and words which she stuck on the 'word wall' on a weekly basis. Then about the 'naughty room' which was essentially the conservatory but with the door closed. A threat rarely used but something to fix their behaviour if required. Effectively she was a mum, nursery teacher, school teacher, cook, cleaner and guide to them all at once. Her home was their first university and launching pad for life. And there was only one chance to get this right.

This was all old news to her husband whom she updated every day. He only listened to it because he did not have the energy to resist as the day normally wore him out. In any case his children normally attacked him with hugs and kisses and complaints when he came home and he took them for a couple of hours messing around in the 'play room'.

The Priest was extremely pleased to hear all this. The family did not need much guidance as they were doing a great job. But at these times encouragement, reassurance and reflection is also guidance. It is both necessary and important.

"We forget our own childhood," commented the Priest. "We think we have been raised ourselves without any input from our parents. But in fact there has been a massive and significant participation - time, struggle and effort. Changing nappies and feeding is one of the easiest things to do when raising children. But that isn't raising them, that is looking after them. Moulding a young person's character. Teaching them right and wrong. Showing them how to respect humanity and respect the environment. Teaching them to care and to recognise fairness and justice and showing them how to deal with difficulty and disappointment. Showing them how to be good children and good parents. To be honest and decent. Bringing home an honest living on which to live."

The Priest then shifted his weight slightly and continued. The couple were silent and focused. "Schooling just educates, it does not teach character or morality as modern schooling does not know what to teach in these areas. Modern morals are extremely flexible. Right and wrong changes every day and every year and with every journalist and every government."

Some of this went over their heads but the message struck a deep chord and had to be explored further.

"What's the best advice you can give," asked the mother, "for giving a child all these things?"

The Priest smiled and settled even further back in his chair. It was indeed a powerful question, deserving of a powerful answer. "I asked my honourable mother this very same question," he answered. "And she said to me to follow children like you are their shadow. Know where they are, who they are with, what they are saying doing and even what they are thinking. Lots of love and lots of structure and discipline when required, but also teaching by example."

Both were listening carefully to the Priest as their minds and hearts were being filled with this potent and powerful knowledge. Only a few words spoken, but rich in meaning and even richer in action.

# 11. The Professional

The letter was signed "Your humble and obedient servant."
It was over one hundred and twenty years and was a letter from
a contractor and businessman to a rich aristocrat about a rather
large mansion and garden development on the Welsh coast.

The Priest had travelled to Wales to meet a family who had
bought a nice farm and converted it to their dwelling. The
owner was a senior IT consultant and was making good money,
hence the purchase and conversion. Working mostly from
home, he had set up a very nice and spacious office and had
rented some of his fields to local farmers. The refurbishment
had been undertaken to a very high standard, taking him a good
five years and triple his expected budget.

The owner had found an old letter in a pile of documents in
his basement which he was in the process of restoring. He was
amused by this one which he showed the Priest. "Do you see,"
he said, pointing at the signature. "It says, 'Your humble and
obedient servant'. Can you believe how people used to sign.
So humbly, but also truthfully I suppose. Because at that time
slavery was rife."

The Priest took the letter and read it carefully. It was written
extremely respectfully but also surprisingly well and technically
concise and accurate. A good summary of the business plan,
main project milestones and the essential engineering and
architectural aspects and features. It did mention
accompanying drawings but these were not with the letter. The
writer appeared an accomplished entrepreneur and engineer

and his writing style was confident and appealing. He was able to raise finance and appeared to have the technical and management skills to get things done.

"But nothing has changed," commented the Priest. "Being a professional is actually just that. A humble and obedient servant. A professional slave. We have inherited this submissiveness and it is still rampant in our world."

The IT consultant was surprised at this comment. Being very proud of his subject and very successful, he wanted to answer that comment as he didn't agree with it. "Surely not?" he questioned, "no-one ever signs letters like that anymore, they would just be laughed at. We are certainly no-one's 'humble and obedient servants'."

The Priest looked around the large lounge they were sitting in. Spacious, bright, lots of natural light, contemporary but with large old oak beams protruding lower than the ceilings and spanning the entire room. They were proudly announcing their permanent, historical presence in the present, refurbished world. The patio doors were essentially a large number of single doors on a rail that were able to fold back to present a large rectangular opening onto the decking. This could be used for the rare summer days occasionally experienced in Wales. The field under and behind the decking was impressive with hills rolling away towards the horizon. In actual fact they were not 'rolling' anywhere, they were absolutely still, but there you go. The illogical use of verbs for the sake of literary decoration always manages to escape an honest grammatical analysis.

"What IT institute do you belong to?" asked the Priest.

The IT consultant mentioned two names of prestigious IT related institutions and he declared them proudly as if to announce his membership, rather than just mention it. He was certainly no one's slave or servant.

The Priest again admired the view from the windows of the stationary hills. It was a pleasant place to sit and discuss. The lowered oak beams though, were totally out of place. A plain, flush ceiling would have been adorable. But these hugely thick beams that were knotted, twisted, discoloured and slightly deformed were quite an eyesore and totally out of place. They were not performing any structural role whatsoever, just decorative and for show; announcing how environmentally friendly the owners were.

"And what did you have to do in order to join these prestigious institutions?" enquired the Priest.

The consultant then began to list out the work experience, examinations, interviews, assessments and years of hard work before being recognised as a Member. Then academic papers, charity work and business successes in order to be recognised as a Fellow.

"So," commented the Priest, "There were many stages before you became one of the chief slaves of the institution."

"I am not a slave of the institution," protested the consultant, "I am a professional of the institution."

"Yes," responded the Priest calmly, "but in order to have become a Member or a Fellow, there were a number of stages that you had to pass and then get discussed amongst your peers before being nominated."

"Yes of course," the consultant replied.

"And in this you had to obey all the rules of the profession and to promote IT and the work of the institution."

"Yes of course," agreed the consultant again.

"So," continued the Priest, "rules had to be obeyed, you could not change your profession, you could not work against it, in fact you were tied to it and its rules as a slave is tied to his Plantation. And you can never get your freedom if you wish to remain a Fellow. You are branded for life."

"No," protested the consultant again, although this time he was not able to offer any counter arguments. It was true. If he wished to remain a Fellow, he would be required to continue to obey the professional rules.

"And in the case of your profession or job, you are in the same position. You must get to work on time, leave on time, your hours are monitored, your workload is checked, every minute is practically accounted for and if there is a slump in the market, then you could lose your job at any stage, irrespective of your loyalty or amount of service and sacrifice you have made. Even if you have brought in a huge amount of business, at the end of the day you are not treated as a human and the politics in business is as dirty as in government."

Now there was a pause as the consultant started to think. Yes, he had sacked people in this manner without feeling or humanity. But he had no choice as one can only pay what the company earns.

"Even your holidays are controlled and sometimes even your evenings and weekends. The contract you sign is one thing, but the unsigned and unwritten contract is also signed by you and expected from you, otherwise you are considered disloyal."

Again, no comment. Just thinking.

"We are slaves to the system, not the other way around. We serve as slaves and we are in professional bondage as slaves. Treated as beasts of burden in our professions. Just earning enough to buy our house, car and our food. Pay for our scheduled holidays. In fact, our whole life is controlled. Slavery and financial control through and through."

"No," said the consultant, "it's not the same as slavery of the past."

"No indeed," replied the Priest, "in this Plantation, we are sometimes free to choose our own master, but the masters of the plantation are themselves also slaves. They want the power to hire and fire, but can be fired themselves. Surely the 'corner office' can't be that great a prize?"

The consultant laughed. He was beginning to appreciate the content and direction of the discussion.

"We need to live a balanced life," said the Priest, "where we can divide up our time between work, family and ourselves. Our professions don't encourage that at all - in fact most of the time they don't allow it. Work hard and play hard is the motto in this civilised world. That's not a very civilised ethos."

A pause in the discussion as the consultant had the expression of a light coming on in his head. He was beginning to agree.

"But then we are all slaves," he commented. "No matter whom we work for or what we do. We are all slaves."

"Yes," replied answered the Priest. "That's my point. We are all slaves. We are working in our respective Plantations for our respective slave masters. Being a professional is being a humble and obedient servant to someone, isn't it? We may not write it any more in our letters, but it is a state of fact. We are slaves to our professional institutions and slaves to our companies and our bosses. If we own these companies then we are slaves to our clients and if we don't own them, then we are slaves to our shareholders."

With this the Priest sat back as the discussion required a short intermission. Again the Priest admired the clouds that were drifting lazily across the rolling, stationary hills. Clouds are remarkable. Infinitely diverse, always changing, each one different, existing for only a short period of time and each shape beautiful, random but delicately designed. Made up of billons of water droplets, these common, unappreciated and insignificant, these fluffy giants providing our planet with life as well as beauty and shade. A picturesque scene of a moving tapestry in the sky.

"It's more than that," continued the Priest. "We are so naive that we can even become slaves of Donkeys."

"Eh what?" asked the professional, extremely surprised. "Slaves to Donkeys? Nooo," he blurted out sniggering and unintentionally snorting. Now he felt a little bit embarrassed, hopeful that nothing had come out of his nose. He quickly reached for a tissue from his pocket.

"You've heard the story of the Donkey haven't you?" asked the Priest.

The professional shook his head in intrigue as he wiped his nose with the tissue.

The Priest began. "A father & son both ride a donkey into a village. Villagers complain to them that both of them should not be on the donkey as it's cruel. So only father rides the donkey into the next village and the son walks. People in this second village then complain that the father is unkind to the son as he is riding while his son walks. So they swap, and in the next village, villagers complain that the son is being disrespectful as he is making his father walk. So in the fourth village, they are both walking. Villagers then complain that they have a perfectly good donkey and it's not being used. Now they are confused and they sit and think what to do. So the son has a suggestion. 'Why don't we carry the donkey?' he asks."

The professional and Priest both laughed. "Yes," said the professional, "I understand. Slaves to a Donkey. We have become Donkeys as well," and he sniggered (but no snorting this time).

"That's not all," continued the Priest. "There are many lessons we can learn here. The first is that whatever we do, we should expect silly comments. The second is that there are always people around to confuse and misguide us. We should also make *du'a* not to have a son like this. Also, it appears that the donkey comes out the winner here."

They were both laughing with each other as they both related the story to the discussion, the sarcasm and the light heartedness. All the while the picturesque clouds just drifted past.

# 12.  *Many Little Things*

"It hurts," he said in tears, and I don't know what to do."

The Priest was sitting calmly and relaxed, leaning back in his chair, waiting patiently for his time to speak. He had cracked this young man who was now bearing his soul. It didn't take long, just a few minutes as the Priest knew exactly the route to his pain and anguish.

"Please help me," he pleaded. "It's awful."

The issue was one of mad and desperate love. So deeply was this young man infatuated that he had even contemplated suicide. So his family had dragged him along to see the Priest. Fortunately for them he was subdued and quiet at this time. Unfortunately though, he still had suicide on his mind as the whispering was powerful, taking full advantage of his vulnerability.

The issue was largely due to his youth, inexperience and powerful hormones. He had been rejected by a shy and beautiful girl at his University whom he had been harassing. As a result of all this she had changed her University, he had been threatened by her parents, and he had messed up his year. The writing was on the wall and he was about to be kicked out. His mother was in a state of shock and his father was livid. Luckily the Priest had calmed them down, and here they were. Parents were in the next room and the young man was now talking to someone.

As he was now out of touch with her, he had spiralled into depression. A dark, deep chasm with no way out. Any help offered by others had already been rejected. This was the young man's temporary madness. A deadly and dangerous kind of insanity which required to be dealt with and dealt with urgently. The Priest was willing and he was ready. He let him say what he had to say. A mad and overwhelming sense of grief, loss and sorrow filled his eyes – and his eyes were windows onto his soul. The Priest would have to reach into the depths of his being and gently pull him back into some sort of reality. This would be a surgical process and like all surgeries, it could easily go wrong. If at any point the young man would give up, the world could lose him and he would never return. However, the anaesthetic was being prepared and the spiritual operation was about to start.

"You say you love?" asked the Priest, as he started to inject the sedative. "Please, explain what love is?"

The young man looked up. A stare of utter helplessness and a deep, deep depression. He had resigned himself to his fate and although he was speaking, he could see no way out and did not want out. Who could help him and why should they? No-one could help, so he had resigned himself to defeat. He was ready to surrender and to be subjugated by his weaknesses.

"Please," encouraged the Priest, "what is love?" The anaesthetic was now completely delivered and was about to take effect. This question was for the patient to count to 'ten'.

"Its madness," he answered. "It's rubbish. It's unreal and not real. It doesn't exist. It's dishonest and unfair." Tears started to run down his cheeks. Words could no longer come out. Helpless and alone. Every part of his being totally depressed. His life felt empty, devoid of all his previous hopes and aspirations. "Its pain," he spluttered. "Just pain. Sadness and pain."

The Priest allowed a pause. It was important as his old self had to be put to sleep so that his new and fresh consciousness could begin. The medicine was slowly beginning to take hold.

Tea and coffee were bought in as a strange normality tried to show itself. The spring sun was setting and long shadows started appearing in the Priest's office. His desk lamp, with a rich, green glass shade was glowing warmly, reflecting peacefully off the leather writing pad - perfectly flush and recessed into the-top of the desk. The spiralling subtle gold patterns in the corners indicating tradition, antiquity and soundness. Solid English Mahogany to the untrained eye and cheap eastern Pine to the trained. A dark varnish veiling the fraud as frugality banished authenticity.

"Are you able to answer the question?" the Priest asked quietly again.

The young man looked up with his sad, helpless and lonely eyes. His emotions anesthetised and brain in and uncontrollable shutdown.

"No," he answered, expressing a vast emptiness.

"Shall I tell you what your pain is?" he asked the young man rhetorically. "Shall I tell you what is happening and shall I tell your solution?" The Priest paused. He did not expect an answer and the silence spoke loudly and clearly. "It's not love," he said. "It is lust. Not love, but lust. Lust is chemical, love is spiritual."

The young man looked sombre and dejected as the Priest repeated the diagnosis again. It hadn't sunk in and it wouldn't sink in so quickly. This process would take a number of months, but at least it had started. The young man would have this phrase reverberating whenever he would think of committing suicide. It was the way it was placed into his mind and heart. Surgically, sensitively and deliberately.

As the weeks passed, the healing process continued. Suicide had been prevented. Now the task was to make him slowly let this 'lust of his life' go. This would then allow this young man to breathe again and to re-enter a cognisant world.

"I wish to discuss beauty with you," began the Priest. "Your longing for this young lady is purely based upon the false notion of beauty. Beauty of the face and body, rather than beauty of the character and beauty of the heart. An illusive beauty; a mirage."

The young man was listening. There were signs of weariness on his face and still a sadness and loss,. Although he had improved enormously. He had still tried several times to contact this young lady and now had been served a harassment notice by the police. He was still depressed, too much to get on with his life but not enough to do something mad or crazy. In this respect the Priest had pulled him out of his drowning pool, in which many poor souls maintain their existence and in which some even end it.

"There was an amazing and beautiful woman," the Priest began, "a long, long time ago. People used to pause and stare at her incredible beauty. They became hypnotised when they saw her. Her voice was mesmerizing and her movements exquisite and full of grace. Her figure, face, looks, just perfect. She was simple, pure and shy. Many offered her marriage, many large sums of money and her guiding Priest had to protect her from the evil eyes and from the bad intentions of the people." The Priest paused as they both sipped their drinks.

"One day, she approached her Priest and begged him to take away her beauty. She said that it was upsetting for her whole family as some young individuals had become mad over her and had threatened her and her parents. Rich and powerful people had also succumbed to her graces and presence. Some of them had vowed that she would be theirs or no-ones. The Shaikh had also been contacted and threatened in order for him to use his influence on the beautiful girl and her family. So the Shaikh decided to act. He decided to sell her beauty."

The young man was intrigued. He was himself beginning to listen to this story as it touched his own existence over the past few months.

"So," the Priest continued, "the sale was arranged and many, many people turned up. The community was amazed that the Priest was actually undertaking this sale. He was known as a wise and powerful person, upholding truth, protecting the innocent and being strong against injustice. Before the sale started, he said that he wished everyone to see the woman's beauty, which he was selling. After all, they should see what they wish to buy. He also corrected people who thought that he was selling the beautiful young lady. He said clearly that he was selling only her beauty. After all, isn't that what people were spellbound by?"

"But," began the young man, "how did.. how does... surely her beauty is a part of her. How can you take away someone's beauty and then sell it?"

The Priest smiled as this young man had also assumed that she was being sold.

"She became sick," the Priest explained. Her sickness lasted a week. She vomited and she had diarrhoea. Her health left her and she slowly became pale, weak and began to look old. She was told to vomit in a bucket. Then the great *Shaikh* announced that he would not only show the girl to all those who were desperate to see her, but also that her beauty would be sold separately. So they gathered. This time was at the peak of her illness, after which she would get better. So the great *Shaikh* showed her to the people. They were extremely anxious to see, desperate and curious but all they saw was a sick, weak, feeble and a pathetic woman. Cheeks pale and sucked in, skin wrinkled and skeletal limbs. Ugly. There was an outcry. 'Where has her beauty gone? Was it a deceit?' The great *Shaikh* again explained that he had taken out her beauty just as he promised and he was going to sell it. Anyone who was interested could see it and make an offer. So they cued to marvel at this miracle. Clearly her beauty had been taken out, just as the great *Shaikh* had promised. And then they were presented with a bucket. The very same one in which the once beautiful young lady had vomited. Because her beauty had definitely left her body, her vomit and diarrhoea must have taken it away. Her beauty was certainly for sale but would not be bought by anyone."

The Priest paused and looked at the young, sick man in front of him. He was taking most of it in. But this medicine would still take time to work. Not days or weeks, but months. He then decided to add a few words to make sure he realised and understood.

"When you love someone for his or her appearance, it is not love but lust and attraction. When you love someone for his or her intelligence, it is not love but admiration. When you love someone for money, it is not love but profit. When you love someone for the sake of Allah - that is sincerity and that is true love. True beauty is not of the body, but it is of the heart and soul. Bodily beauty can be looked at as filth and foul."

The young man listened quietly as the Priest continued. "Life is full of joys and agonies, ecstasies and miseries; broken rules and desperate chances; glorious failures and famous victories. We just have to get up and battle on. That is what we are designed to do and that is what we are destined to do."

Now it was clarified, his confusion and apprehension was the same confusion and apprehension of all those who had been in front of this great *Shaikh* of the past. The event that occurred so many years ago in a different land in a different culture and a different generation, but it was being repeated. The emotions and the lesson were also being repeated. In this way such examples live forever so that such lessons can be learned forever.

The priest continued: "We are a fusion of soul and clay, of spirituality and dust, emotions and matter, reality and dreams. In such a mix there will inevitably be struggle and there will definitely be difficulty. We must revert back to clay to survive."

# 13.  The Shopping List

What a Palaver.  The children were indeed growing up and growing up fast.  Their brains were engaged and making new and exciting connections with every conversation, sometimes with every sentence.

"Will you miss mum and daddy when they go away?" asked his big sister.

"No, because I have their picture," her younger brother answered sincerely.  "And I woke up early this morning because I had to have my breakfast," he declared.

They were both engaged in some sort of colouring mission with different crayons and pencils scattered about on the floor in front of them.  There was a hint of order but more a message of chaos in their arrangement as they coloured in the empty pictures with a sense of urgency.  Their parents were busy packing upstairs and the Priest was quietly reading his holy beads as they played in front of him.  The parents wished the Priest to bless their spiritual journey to the holy lands, and had begged him to come to their house to see them off.  Of course, he had agreed.

"Did you wash your face before you had your breakfast?" she asked in a motherly way.

"Yes," he answered, colouring the tree a strange orange.

"Well, I don't know why you did that because you are only going to get dirty again."  Her innocent logic was flawless.

"What time is it?" she asked, "because mummy and daddy have to leave in ten minutes."

"Its twenty three twenty eight," he replied, using fragments of his memory from someone recently telling him the time.

"Did you tell mummy about your injewy?" she asked him, referring to his injured knee, which she had struck by mistake.

"Yes," he replied, "but I had to speak fast as she was busy."

"What did she say?" she asked.

"She told me I don't listen and a few other things which I don't remember," he answered.

"Have you done the shopping list for mummy and daddy?" she asked.

"Yes," he replied, "It's in my book," as he then stopped is colouring and ran to his book. He grabbed it, took out a piece of paper and gave it to his big sister.

Like a little mum she took it to examine it as she saw her mother examine any list produced by her father. She read through it item by item. "colliflower, marjreen, qoocumber, conflaiks, milk, fizzi dwinks, tomarto saws and tee." She paused and then said, "You have spellt 'sauce' wrong. You need to practice your spelling. And you missed out other things. She grabbed her pencil and started writing while her brother looked over her shoulder. She read out the items as she wrote them, putting her little teacher hat on. "Braed, cakes, fish fingers, cwips, sofa, 2 letere water bottle." She paused as she began to think of more items.

"What about a new car?" asked her younger brother. So she wrote 'car' as well as they remembered their parents arguing over the number of times it broke down. "You need to write 'car that doesn't bwake down'," he shouted eagerly, and then, "Write slowly as I can't read very fast."

As she was writing, the boy suddenly came up with a question. "What would you do without - your knees or your elbows?"

His sister continued to write and to decorate some of the list with pictures. She had heard the question and thought it was a good one. "Errmm, my knees," she replied, "as I can walk with straight legs but I won't be able to write without my elbows."

'Clever,' the boy thought. 'That's clever. I think I will also say that next time somebody asks me.'

The Priest was still quiet in front of the children. He was watching them play and talk while listening to the parents panicking, arguing and packing upstairs. Clearly the parents were stressed out, while the children were totally unconcerned except with what was directly in front of them and ahead of them. Their innocence flowed and glowed around them.

"What shall I wite now?" asked the boy.

"Now you should write the most important things you should do. All the good things." Clearly, she had remembered this activity from a previous session with her mum.

"Like what?" asked the boy.

"Like being good!" she exclaimed.

"Okay," he said eagerly as he took a new sheet of paper from his little pile, lined it up and began writing with his focused writing face.

1. Work: School Work / home Work!

2. chors!

3. polite!

4. maners!

(Clearly, it appears that he had just learned the use of the exclamation mark.)

5. Learn:Gography, Chemisry, Litracy and maths!

6. DOn't give up!

7. Trust Peeple!

8. Always try your best!

10. always Share!

11. Never Snatch!

12. Never be craul!

13. Always be kind!

14. eat healthily!

15. exersiZe!

16. Never give up!

17. Do not braig!

18. Do not say swears!

19.  Don't be bored after your birthday!

His sister was all over the list and started correcting, criticising and confusing.

After another half-hour or so, the parents came down, flustered, tired and stressed out.  Then they were bombarded by their two kids showing them what they had done and each complaining about the other.  The parents showed a minor interest – a well practised act, while trying to avoid hitting them with the various bags now piling up in the small hallway.  The son tried to pick one of the suitcases up when his father wasn't looking but just managed to move the leather handle up and down.  'Crikey,' he thought, 'daddy is strong.'

After another thirty minutes or so of loading the car, then the father's handkerchief came out, wiping his brow whilst his wife was busy with the kids, looking at their colourings and shopping list.  By now their aunty had come to look after them and she would take them into her own house once everyone had said their farewells.

Now the parents and the Priest were alone in the front room.  The children were in the back room with their aunty being kept busy.

The mother was quietly sobbing as the Priest spoke to both of them, softly and delicately.  He knew how long it had taken them to save up for this.  He also knew how difficult it was to leave their children for a full month.  He also knew the problems they would be facing with their trials and tribulations.

It is said that the longest journey starts with the first step. It is also said that life is a continuous journey of tests, battles and joys. For the parents, this journey began with a pure intention many years ago, in fact, on the day they were married. Since then they tried to save but had to buy a house, car and to look after their growing family. However, with the Priests guidance, they were now in this fortunate position, to fulfil a life-long dream, ambition and obligation. They were both sat quietly, listening to a history lesson and a future lesson.

"This is a journey of a lifetime. The rules and regulations you know - the secrets you do not know."

They listened quietly and attentively. Like little children, soaking in the advice, because now it mattered. A lecture delivered at any other time would have been listened to but not absorbed. Now every word was swallowed, every idea digested, every teaching subsumed. The guidance was in Urdu as this is the language of their thought and of their spirit.

"The most important lesson is to be extremely patient as with a lot of people around you there will be tests, deceptions, and tests again. You must be careful not to lose your temper. Whatever is written will happen and what is not will not. Supplication, even for the most minor of things is recommended as this will ease so much difficulty. You must focus on '*Ibadah*, day time and night time. There must be no compromise. Leave mundane shopping till the last day. Remember your dreams and appreciate the small events that will take place for your benefit. Do not reflect on the negative as that can only change with effort combined with supplication. It can change and it will change."

And then the final, wonderful piece of advice, before they left on their spiritual journey of a lifetime.

"When you return, it will be like all your stresses, worries and your sins have fallen away as leaves fall from a tree. A new life and existence. Beneficial for yourself, your children and for all those around you. This blessed journey is one where you must take with you your personal list of essential requirements that you need to acquire in your life and beyond. A list that includes all goodness for your loved ones as well, past, present and future. And you need to ask for all your items – each and every one. In this way, your present can be blessed and your future fulfilled. The most important shopping list you will ever make. We make many plans and designs for material things, but rarely design our lives and our futures. We make lists of things to be bought but not a list of what we actually need. Materiality distracts us and distresses our souls, but inner richness is via other means and once received it is fulfilling and satisfying. We grant ourselves the present but deny ourselves our future. Thus we miss many opportunities for great blessings and rewards. This is your opportunity to design your future and to benefit. Avail yourselves, avail yourselves."

With that advice they parted.

# 14.   Heart of the Matter

It was clear that the topic was the human heart, or rather the human, spiritual heart. The Priest was sitting quietly having asked the question. Now he was waiting for the answer. The question was direct, succinct and searching. The student knew that it was a reflective question whereby he was being asked to bear his heart and soul as this was demanded by the nature of the question.

"It's not just a piece of flesh..." began the student and then paused for thought. "It is a very special and extremely important part of our being as it determines life and survives death."

At this point the Priest smiled. A very faint one so as not to warn the student what was going to occur next. Was he going to tear him apart, intellectually and spiritually? Or was he going to just teach him? The answer was a good one. So this session was beginning well. The humility and training were beginning to kick in.

"It decides our fate," he continued, "at many levels. It houses the worst and also the best. It is the seat of love, wisdom and knowledge and the depository of hate, greed and anger. It is linked to our souls, minds and our faith. It determines intentions, good or bad and colours our deeds. It flourishes with patience, compassion and acceptance. It is hardened with anger and haste and it is destroyed with arrogance, corruption and comforts."

The student paused. Pleased with his answer and hoped his teacher was also.

"Are you are happy with your answer?" asked the Priest.

"Only if you are happy with it," the student responded using a honey-trap reply.

The Priest paused and decided to rip into his logic a little and to spring the trap. A honey-trap, no matter how refined or crude - and crude in this case. "No, but you are happy with your answer aren't you?" he asked again. Now the question could not be ignored and it could not be circumvented.

The student knew that he couldn't use the same reply. The trap did not work and now the Priest was setting a bear trap for him. He had to be careful. "I believe it is a correct reply, yes," he answered.

"No," responded the Priest. "It is only correct if your happiness with the reply is your ego being happy and proud - or happiness of another type."

"I don't believe it is my ego," responded the student.

"So what type of happiness is it?" asked the Priest.

The student paused. This was difficult. He felt he was being cornered. He searched his brain frantically for an answer.

"You won't find your answer in your brain," stated the Priest almost immediately.

This was now getting scary. He then decided to search into his heart. He was working hard. His breathing became deeper as his brain started utilising more of its capacity. Then he thought he found the answer. "It's a happiness of satisfaction, and not one of pride," he stated, although he wasn't sure.

"A happiness of satisfaction *is* one of pride," responded the Priest. "If you are happy with yourself and your answer then you are proud. Is that correct or false?"

This was getting worse. The student was thinking even faster. Almost in a panic. Then he remembered and he calmed down. He started breathing deeply and normally. His body was now calm as was his heart and his soul. Now the knowledge started to flow. Not from his knowledge, but from his beating heart and his searching soul. So what was the answer?

"So what is the answer?" pressed the Priest.

Still quiet and breathing regularly and gently, the student responded. "It *is* the happiness of satisfaction," he began. "The satisfaction that I am being taught. The satisfaction that I am learning. The satisfaction that I am truthful. The satisfaction that if I am wrong, I can be corrected. The satisfaction that I am grateful for all these things."

The Priest looked at the student. He was going to have to travel into his brain even deeper and explore the complex intricacies of his thinking using this answer as a means. Answering correctly was not enough. Answering with inner truth and reality was required. "So why are you satisfied?" he asked.

His answer came swiftly: "Because of my desire to learn the truth and to help others. To enrich people and to give them hope and peace. Only if my heart is satisfied can I make others satisfied."

And so the questioning went on and on and on. Probing and examining his thought processes more and more. Forcing him to assess and analyse and understand. Thus the student was learning to read himself and his heart. It was intense and demanding.

After a good hour, the student felt battered and drained and the Priest was totally fresh. When the Priest felt the student's mind and energy had been completely sapped by the interrogation, only then did he pause.

The Priest was looking at the student who appeared calm but drained. He decided to conclude the meeting with this now empty, tired mental shell in front of him. Almost brain dead and exhausted. This will do for this time. So he decided to preach and also to reward him with beautiful and sincere teachings. "Ones heart is a fusion of clay and emotion. It can be enlightened and strengthened by spirituality but also destroyed by so many things. If it is troubled, patience heals it. If blessed with too much happiness it forgets to be cautious and becomes neglectful. Freedom from difficulty makes it proud. Eagerness weakens it and anger destroys its fabric. Wealth makes it poor and continuous victory fills it with arrogance and causes it to fail. Only when true peace is allowed to enter can the heart find satisfaction and true strength. Any excesses will cause it injury except one excess - the Creator's remembrance. One has to look deeply in order to discover whether this is indeed the case. I invite you to look into yours."

The student paused and looked a little shocked. He was nervous and worried, but his instruction had been given and he was obliged to follow. 'But what a request?' he thought. 'Offered to so few, but required of me.'

In fact, he was allowed to follow as he had been given permission. Besides, he had no energy to resist, although enough to appreciate. So he closed his eyes and peered directly into his heart. He found himself in a maze. It was challenging, but eventually he found his way. He was focused, determined and curious. When he looked really deeply and eventually found his path, he saw someone else already there. It was the Priest, sitting quietly, humbly and peacefully. He was looking at the student and he was smiling.

# 15.   The Baggage Handler

What a cruel young man he was. His mum was crying and he was still insulting her. Using her natural, strong emotional attachment against her.

"You are the cruellest mother in the world," he protested. You don't listen to anything I say and you have never looked after me. Cruel and evil through and through."

The Priest was sitting behind his desk and mother and son were sitting opposite him. It was a surgery day and the Priest was seeing client after client. These were number seven that morning. The office was bathed by the light of a faintly clouded sun on a warm spring day. His numerous books on their shelves boasting their contents, each competing with their decorative spines.

His mum continued to sob in embarrassment as well as hurt. It was a miracle that she had persuaded him to come with her. It was his arrogance though rather than his mum pleading that persuaded him. 'Who was this stupid Priest anyway whom his mum keeps going to for help and support?' He was curious and also wanted to dominate his mother completely.

The Priest sat quietly. The mother was hoping he would shout at him and tell him off in some way. She was hoping for a miracle. Ever since her divorce her son had changed and her daughters had become distant. She was alone, hurt and confused, being battered from all sides.

"I just work like a slave for my children," she sobbed, tears falling gently into her dupatta which she used to wipe her eyes every now and again. "I have to earn the money and cook and clean and raise them when they should be looking after me." Her breathing now in short, sharp bursts. She was mentally exhausted and felt emotionally abused. A worthless human, a lonely and pathetic woman and a useless mother. She was at the lowest she had ever felt. A wounded heart and an injured soul. In pain and continuously bleeding with no respite. It was painful and it was pointless.

The Priest was quite upset at this. He had always taught and guided people to respect their parents without compromise and without condition. This was extremely distressing but he did not allow his feelings to distract him. He used them to focus. There was some good in the son and there were reasons for his abuse and his bullying. He had missed his absent father which contributed to his frustration. However, the constant whispering was more serious and was having a huge and continuous impact.

The Priest watched the performance like a member of an audience in a Theatre. Unperturbed, as if he had seen this play dozens of times. He breathed calmly and regularly, watching this son abuse his fragile and innocent mother. But he had to wait for the right moment. And then it came. Now the tempo would be changed and the main part of the Play could begin. A series of life changing and profound scenes were about to be directed in the Priests small office. Truly a spiritual stage where the hearts of life's actors are uncovered and called to account.

"Could I please ask you a question?" he asked the son.

The son paused. His mother too distraught to look up. The son looked up at the Priest. His eyes full of hatred and anger. The whispering continuous. The Priest had broad shoulders and well built upper body with kind and merciful eyes. The son's anger subsided just a little, but he had also come to challenge this man. His mother's emotional destruction could only be complete once he destroyed this guiding light she kept returning to. Her beacon of hope and her salvation needed to be extinguished. Now was the moment he would take the Priest on and he would win, as he always did with his mum.

"I don't know who you think you are," he began. "You have no idea what my situation is at home and how cruel this woman is to me. She does not love her children, she has no education and she just comes to see you like you are some free psychiatrist. You are a waste of time just like her. You haven't helped her one bit."

The son sat back in his chair. Happy. Let's see this Priest answer him. 'No one would have dared speak to this person before. 'I have', he thought, 'and in front of my stupid mum'.

The Priest looked calm and relaxed. Completely untroubled. "Actually," the Priest began, "it was never my intention to help your mother. I have never really actually helped her."

"Then why does she come to see you?" he shouted at him. "Why?" 'I am winning,' he thought, 'I have him on the run.'

The Priest looked at this young man in front of him. Full of anger and looking for a fight. He breathed in deeply and

127

relaxed into his chair. He then decided to start to help this young man in need. "It was always my intention to help her family," the Priest replied calmly. "Her family is her children and of course you."

"Well you haven't done a good job have you!" he shouted back, leaning forward a little as if to throw his words at the Priest.

Then without warning, the Priest stood up suddenly. The son's heart skipped a beat and he stopped breathing for a few seconds. He saw the Priest's mighty stature just a few feet away from him, standing up behind the desk. His powerful chest and arms suited his wide and tall frame. He did indeed appear dominant and immovable. A solid wall of chest and muscle betwixt his wide shoulders. The Priest stayed for a few seconds, unmoved. His expression cold and powerful, eyes menacing and invasive. His soul bright and blinding. A force not to be reckoned with; authoritative and dominating; without fear and without weakness. Then, again with no warning, he adjusted his seat and slowly sat down, looking straight at the son. A stare of serenity and strength. There appeared to be a threat and then it just disappeared – or rather it had retreated back into the Priest's body. The son was confused and he was scared.

"You say that I haven't done a good job," he stated calmly. "But you see, I haven't started yet. I am actually going to start now. On you."

This time the son was silent. He was afraid. He was now arguing with a powerful man, and not his weak, little mum. A

128

stranger whom he didn't know, and who appeared not to be interested in argument. Remaining cool, calm and collected. Immensely strong. Dominating. Unafraid but one who appeared in total control. A powerful persona, physically and spiritually controlling the room and the humans and non-humans in the room. Even the whisperer was scared.

The Priest looked at this young man. Full of hate and anger. His moral compass pointing in all the wrong directions. He was going to make it point north and sort out his confused spiritual, magnetic field.

The son collected himself. His arrogance kicked in to direct him what to say. "So when are you going to start?" asked the son unpleasantly. He had plucked up the courage to finally speak but his voice was shaky. His mother kept quiet having no strength to get involved.

"I've already started," replied the Priest, extremely softly.

"Well I don't believe you," responded the son, shrugging his shoulders and turning away from the Priest. "You haven't started. You know nothing." At this point, he crossed his legs and turned slightly away to hide his fear. But his foot had begun shaking and a layer of sweat just above his upper lip.

The Priest remained silent. Breathing slowly and peacefully. Extremely relaxed. His face now took on a slightly serious look as he leaned a little forward and almost whispered: "I would like to talk to about your dream you had last night." He then relaxed back into his chair. He had lit the fuse, and it had begun to burn. He was in full attack mode. Air, land and sea, all in unison. Short, sharp, simple and sweet. He had declared war on the sons pride, arrogance and frustrations and also was attacking all the dark forces that were foolish enough to be present. No matter how much wisdom evil thinks it has, it is always annihilated by the truth.

The son now froze for a good few seconds. He turned and looked at the Priest straight in the eye. He opened his mouth to speak but nothing came out. He began to breathe fast and in short bursts. He closed his mouth but continued to stare at the Priest. His eyes were powerful, laser-like, deep. It was the authority of his look though that pierced through the hatred and anger surrounding the son's heart.

"Yes," said the Priest extremely softly. "I know. I know it all."

The son now turned away. This was not right. 'How did he know?' His foot started shaking more noticeably and his mouth was suddenly extremely dry.

"The man with the terrifying face," said the Priest. "I know who he is and what he is doing to you."

The son now began to feel a chill over his whole body. The description was accurate - frighteningly accurate. This could not be right. 'How could he know?'

The Priest continued. The mum was barely listening. "Very few people in this world can stop him. And yes, he is real. When you felt his hand go through your chest it was real and it was painful. I know."

The son's eyes barely blinked as he listened to every word. Each sentence meeting with no resistance, settling into his head completely. Filling a desperate void. He was overwhelmed that his secret was being revealed and by a complete and utter stranger. Now totally silent; shocked and speechless.

The Priest had paused, allowing time for his words to sink in. Not for dramatic effect, but for dramatic help. "I can help," offered the Priest. "I can stop your pain and the fear. Your headaches, your tiredness. I can help."

The son was now totally quiet. Yes, he was scared and he was hurting. Terrified at night, with any sleep uncomfortable and painful. He was afraid of the dark and at times too terrified to sleep. He was not able to tell anyone, after all, who could help? It was just a dream. But then the hand in his chest? He could still feel the pain. His constantly throbbing head. This was all wrong. He couldn't show any weakness. Who was this Priest?

"Who are you?" asked the son in a raised voice and a slightly panicked tone. "Tell me who you are?" His foot was still shaking.

The Priest paused. Breathing regularly and deeply. Sitting extremely calmly. They were looking at each other. The young man with a look of shock and awe, of wonder and need. For the first time in his life he had made a connection. A proper connection, although one that he had no control over. It was strange and it was also extra-ordinary. His heart had been aching with anger, frustration and fear for so long, he did not know any other way. But now, there was the gentle whisper. A fresh and comforting breeze. An atmosphere of trust. A recognition, an acknowledgement and for the first time - a hope.

It is a sad fact that when a person laughs then the world laughs with them, but when a person cries, he cries alone.

"Who are you?" asked the son again, desperate for an answer. He had been crying alone for so long.

"I am your friend," answered the Priest, "and I will help you... *inshaAllah.*"

# 16.   The Ticking Clock

Tick....tick....tick.  The clock on the mantle-piece tirelessly performed its function.  Without thought or purpose, only function.  Tick...tick...tick.  Its internal mechanism working tirelessly, harmoniously without complaint and without error.  Every part performed its function and the clock would only work if every part fulfilled its purpose.  In this way the universe exists, performs and functions.  Every molecule and every atom, fit for purpose, fixed for purpose and designed for purpose.

The two protagonists for this episode were engaged in a highly focused and challenging discussion.  A battle of the minds and of ideas about truth and wisdom.  Weapons of choice in this fight were knowledge, logic and persuasion.  A struggle in which commitment or perseverance will not win.  No.  One in which truth explained in a rational and methodical way prevails, especially if stated in a manner the other appreciates the most.

"Faith is based upon faith, rather than solid proof?  Surely, this is totally wrong?"  This was the question currently being posed.  "We need proof to believe, it's not correct any other way."

The Priest smiled.  This was a beautiful question and he had a beautiful answer.  "But there are many things we believe in which we cannot see," he responded very calmly.

The Priest had travelled to a south-coast seaside destination to a meeting of different faiths in a church. He had delivered his speech, met the organisers, other speakers and some members of the audience. He had then surprisingly accepted an invitation by someone who had asked a few thoughtful questions and this person had caught his eye. He was a professor of humanities, a self-confessed atheist and they were sitting in his lounge. His wife was also around popping in and out but they more or less had the room to themselves. Their 2.3 children long since grown up and gone leading their own existences. A quiet and mature neighbourhood, well away from the sea, although the sound of seagulls a regular reminder and a pleasant, warm summer evening.

"No," came the reply. "Everything I believe in I have proof for," he confidently stated.

"No," replied the Priest, "you haven't."

So the topics of gravity, quarks, black holes were all discussed. Those things that all know exist but cannot be seen.

"But we can see the effects of all of these," protested the professor. "That's why we know they are there."

"Yes," responded the Priest, "so we can also see the effects of our creator. That's why we know He is there."

And so it continued. Argument and counter argument. Point and counter point. Proof and counter proof. And the clock continued to tick, patiently, predictably and almost silently. When it was heard, it provided a soothing rhythm and comforting distraction. A mechanical heartbeat, tireless, functional, regular. For generations humanity has been obsessed with measuring time. Using the sun for hours and days, the moon for monthly times, with the stars utilised for direction and annual checks. Now with atomic clocks, even accuracy to one-second is far too inaccurate. The demand for precision is such that the theory of relativity can now be proven by these modern masterpieces of philosophy and engineering.

Although we cannot control time, we are fanatical with knowing its exactness and passionate about speaking against it. Complaining when it passes too slowly and complaining when it passes too fast. Every second exists for the briefest of moments, each passing us only once from the future to the past, never to return.

"Life is also a proof," stated the Priest. "And so is death a proof."

"That's not proof," countered the professor. "That is just fact. Life is a fact and death is a fact."

"Yes," answered the Priest. These are facts and these are also proofs. Where facts have fake proofs, these are not facts but lies, but where facts have truth behind them, these are truths. Where does life go after death? All physical laws state that nothing is lost. The laws of thermodynamics, conservation of momentum, action and re-action. They all state that nothing is lost, only transferred. So where does force and reality of life go? "

"Into non-existence," answered the professor. "It vanishes like time."

"So," continued the Priest, "energy gets transferred, momentum is conserved, all actions have opposite reactions, but life? Life just vanishes. Into thin air? Like time? Time just exists for the briefest of moments but we are bound within its limits. Life cannot be compared to time as time is constantly being renewed. How can life just vanish, against all the other laws? And you have no proof professor, just conjecture."

"Yes, but life is different," responded the professor, "it is...well...special." The professor then paused, realising what he had said and still not realising what the Priest had said.

"Do not hide the truth," began the Priest, "or hide from the truth. It comes out soon enough. No matter how deeply it resides, no matter how many veils one uses to try and hide it, it will show itself."

The professor paused. He was against the ropes now and getting jabbed repeatedly. He was struggling. His own words had betrayed his entire philosophy and he had declared his natural realisation of truth and reality. One sentence declared it all. 'Life is special'.

"Yes," continued the Priest. "Life is special. It is unique in creation. It goes beyond the physical laws which we have understood or claim to understand. And it requires someone with the specialist knowledge to teach it to us. If you just consider DNA – the blueprint of our very being. When copying itself it just makes one mistake every billion letters. Is that remarkable or not? A stunning, molecular, double helical structure, made up of combinations of just four base pairs of amino acids. Incredibly stable and resistant to change. A truly dazzling design and an incredible, autonomous mechanism for reproduction and survival. Translating molecular micro management to large scale living organisms."

The clock continued to tick as silence now filled the room. The quiet, continuous mechanical ticking dominating. The professor's brain had to pause and catch up. His philosophy, training and education deserting him in the light of an obvious reality.

The Priest then continued. "Your own philosophical beliefs and teachings shout the existence of God. They shout it loud and they shout it clear."

This was a trap and the professor walked straight into it, confidently and foolishly. "No," he replied. "Not at all." After all, his confidence was based upon his academic teaching of philosophy for most of his adult life.

"Philosophy," explained the Priest, "is an attempt to understand the fundamentals. The fundamentals of nature of knowledge and of life itself, is it not?"

The professor's eyes were wide open staring at the Priest. He was right. Totally correct. He knew this definition, but there was a slight change in the wording and this made him see his subject in a slightly different light. A more interesting and practical light. One which philosophy normally tries to ignore and hide. But the facts had now been exposed.

"Yes," replied the professor, slowly and quietly.

"So," the Priest continued, "why does philosophy exist? Why would we need to discuss our existence and our beliefs?

Why do we need to understand the fundamentals of life? This yearning to understand only exists in humans, not in any other animal on earth. Two monkeys don't sit philosophising with each other over a banana do they? We are different and we are special. Life is special and our questioning also shows something. It shows us that God wants us to find him. He wants us to search and reason and then to discover our purpose and our creation. This reasoning and our own sentient nature cannot have 'evolved' within us, but has been inspired and designed into our fabric. If we evolved from animals then we would just accept without question, just exist to live and die. Unappreciative of time, laws, creation, philosophy and the world around us and beyond us. Your subject itself proves his existence."

Dumb-founded. Speechless. The professor was now blank. His brain had come to an impasse in its thinking. It was weary and tired, not due to this discussion, but due to the quiet battle that had always been fought inside him. And now a light was shining on that conflict and showing all sides, clearly and powerfully. It was forcing him to rethink and re-assess. He was now so grateful to have met this Priest and also fearful he had met this Priest. He needed time to reflect, ponder and think. To philosophise his subject and to philosophise himself. Meanwhile the clock continued to operate – ignorant and unconcerned. Tick...tick...tick.

# 17.  *The Stranger*

It is bizarre when strangers interact, or not interact.  It could be a common issue affecting them that suddenly breaks down all the barriers, allowing speech.  Like danger, an accident, illness, death.  Why is that?  How can so many people travel on a crowded bus or train and never say a word to each other.  All being able to look in different directions at the same time.  Eye contact, well that's not allowed at all.  No way.

One can sit next to a passenger for an entire trans-continental flight and not say a word.  Strangers don't talk to each other.  They don't interact.  It's not allowed.  Strange social creatures we have turned out to be.  If we met in a desert or on a deserted island, we would speak, but in a crowd of people, we do not.  We populate cities in swarms of millions, change the geological landscape and as we become more civilised, and become more and more socially restricted.  Cocooned in our compact, miniature little bodies.  As our wealth increases, our hearts become smaller.

Children on the other hand have to interact and as quickly as they can.  They make friends for the shortest of times but act as if they have been friends for ever.  Willing to be involved, to invade each other's space.  To play meaningless games.  Innocent, free from baggage, their minds fresh.  Their souls slowly becoming stained and contaminated as they grow older.

Even more bizarre then when a stranger offers their help to another stranger.  Not just that, but when a stranger acts in ways they are never expected to act.  To show care.  To show interest. Compassion. Strange sentiments and words even for a family at times let alone strangers.

"How may I help you?" asked the Priest.

The Lobby of this five-star hotel was impressive. It drew people into the premises and gave them a feeling of achievement and ownership. This entire place was there to serve them. They were important - until they checked out. Glistening marble floor tiles, polished daily in rich crimson, black and white, boasting their metamorphic origins. The vast, mushroom chandeliers, cheap imports from China, but looking elegant and flamboyant. Every small, delicate glass crystal, glowing, glistening and reflecting its beauty. The plush sofas, tables and decorations. Also the hugely priced silly artefacts that non-one seemed to buy locked up in their display cases. And the five-star bling to shine the place up. Brass and chrome fittings for the lights, frames and columns, placed for maximum extravagance. Some interior designer obviously had a job-lot left over. Outside the summer sun was rising and it was a fresh, warm morning with just a splatter of cloud.

The Priest had sat down opposite an old woman who appeared a little tired and excited but mostly sad and upset. Her expression demonstrating how complicated and damaging emotions can be. He placed his coffee on the shining, see-through table with large silver and chrome curved, protruding legs. Their ribbed nature adding to their splendour and bulk. He looked at her and smiled. She smiled back a little, and so he had then asked the question that she was waiting for.

The old woman looked at him, confused. This was not how strangers introduce themselves. Aliens shouldn't even talk to you. However, she settled down and studied him carefully. He had a kind face but she would not trust him. She was at the age and maturity that few people could intimidate her. She had nothing to prove or gain or lose any more. No-one in her life had been that sincere to her. She had learned some tough lessons from the tormentors of her past.

"Where did you come from young man?" she asked. "And yes, I do need some help. Actually I need loads of help but I don't think you can help me. I also think I don't want you to help me." She was surprised as to how much she had said but not too worried as what was the point of worrying too much? She had seen it all. Life, death, hurt, joy, happiness, sadness and sorrow. Life was too short and she knew she was nearing the end of hers.

The Priest was still smiling. He took a sip of coffee and then asked, "Why?" in a very soft and gentle manner.

"Well," she began, "you probably don't drink do you?" she asked. This was deliberate because his clothes and appearance presented his religiosity. This should cause him to become upset and hopefully he would leave her alone.

"No" he answered, "but how does that matter?"

That reaction and response was unexpected. So she decided that she would go further. She was not afraid to as her character had become strengthened with every tragedy life had abused her with. "Well because love, it means you live a life so different to mine you won't be able to help. I've already asked

141

my doctor, my Imam, my neighbours and all of my friends. No one has been able to help. So how all of a sudden can you, a total stranger help? No," she responded, shaking her head with a cynical smile. She was confident in her position and predicament.

Another small sip of coffee as the Priest's sincere smile remained. Alluring, pleasant, friendly. "Well," the Priest began, "maybe it's because I'm a stranger that I can help. Maybe it's because I don't drink or take drugs that I can help. Maybe it's because I'm suddenly asking that I can help."

She was silver haired, widowed, well preserved. Frail but spirited. Slow but surely. She had witnessed the joys and pains of life. The triumphs and tribulations, the victories and failures. To have loved and to have lost. Her closest companions now slowly falling at the wayside one by one. Her circle of friends growing ever smaller. Just waiting for her time now. Life for her now was snap, crackle but no 'pop'.

The lobby was a very comfortable place for strangers. To meet but never to know one another. Each marooned in their own existence. Lonely but giving the impression of control and certainty. The Priest was staying over on his way to Scotland. She had come for one of her friend's birthday who was 90 years old. Crikey. She even had a mobile phone but never really charged it up unless she wanted to make a call.

"Okay", she said, not one to walk away from a challenge. "You think I have lost my identity," she began. "But you are wrong. I am proud of it and I have accepted it. As I tell all my Asian friends and family, you have to accept who you are. You

142

can scrub all you want, it won't come off. You are also probably going to tell me to get closer to religion. Well, that won't work either as many Imams and friends have tried. So, tell me, what is my solution?. Actually, tell me my problem first."

So the gauntlet was thrown and the contest about to start. She was dressed in a mixture of eastern and western clothes. Her faith was showing through her style of clothing, but only just. She had lost much of it after the death of her husband. Consoled by memories and artefacts but in tremendous pain and deep distress. Any words of comfort now lame and irrelevant. Falling onto a hurting and hardened heart.

"It's very simple", said the Priest. "You have lost someone really close. Someone you used to talk to. To confide in, to unwind, to walk and talk and hold hands. To laugh and cry. To make fun of each other and of others. You have lost your life's companion. Your soulmate. Your best friend and your best enemy. You put on a massive brave face and you have enormous strength but this struggle is too much to bear. You are now hoping and wishing to die."

The Priest paused. He had spoken tenderly and he had spoken truthfully. He had spoken from his heart, and words from one heart can become imprinted onto another's. She was looking at him eyes wide open. Her pale, wrinkled face slowly becoming wet with two glistening trails. Tears dropped onto her twenty year old shawl where they disappeared into the rich, dark, delicate design. The Priest had recognised her pain and seemed to have witnessed her aching memories.

The Priest continued. "If we look at this world with our physical eyes, we will find it alluring, attractive and permanent. If we look at it with the eyes of our soul we will find it temporary, difficult and dangerous. If we look at it with the eyes of our heart we will find it worthless, dismal and too long." The Priest watched her take it in and he allowed her time for this before he continued, "...and you need to look at this world with your heart."

It was now that she made the connection with him. This was incredible but it was natural. It was unexpected but necessary. Extraordinary but comforting. A deep, rich and fulfilling feeling. Transcending all negativity and helplessness.

She hadn't asked him how he knew, she hadn't asked him who he was, she didn't want to ask any of these as this strange individual had captured her craving and identified and diagnosed her pain. This was her time of rescue and she would grasp the opportunity. "Yes," she said. "I want to die. I want to be with Imran", as her tears continued to gently fall.

His name was Amir but it was an old, old nickname. When he was sent a letter from his grandmother, calling him Imran by mistake. It stuck. A long, boring and irrelevant story, not to be told.

"No," said the Priest. "There is a better way. You can be with him before you die and afterwards as well. That is if you wish. Love is not one, big thing. But it is many little things. It is not association just in our lives on this earth, but in the hereafter as well. It is not just trapped in this life, but extends beyond. It permeates us and binds us and connects us."

144

"No", she said. Then she paused. "Yes. How?" she asked. Now nothing would surprise her as to what this lovely, gentle man would say or do. She believed him and she knew from her innermost being that he spoke the truth.

"It's very simple" said the Priest. "This is what you must do to get back your soul-mate and your tea-mate."

She smiled and cried at the same time. 'Yes. Yes. That is what he was'. She wasn't able to take this intense loneliness. Drinking tea herself. The past six months had been unbearable. Even visiting his grave wasn't helping and her deeply held beliefs were letting her down.

Strangers continued their own little routines of checking in, checking out and checking out others briefly. Conscious that they were being looked at. And when they looked at others they only wished to see if they were looking at them. All appeared busy with a pretend happiness, although rarely smiling. All oblivious to this old woman and her immense pain, gratefulness and now a glimmer of inner bliss.

"You have grown older, but you need to do a little more growing up," the Priest commented.

The Priest then described the few things she needed to do and religious words she needed to read. She followed his advice and then within a few weeks, something amazing. She saw Imran in her dream. She spent all night with him, joking, laughing and drinking tea together. They were in a shaded corner of a giant garden. People around but no one paying attention to them. It was pleasant, happy and relaxing. She hoped she would meet the Priest again. Yes, she had taken his number but somehow deleted it from her mobile.

She had found hope and reconciliation and saw life for what it was. She appreciated the hereafter as it is meant to be. She had made the connection to her situation and had found her role. She used her internal peace to give others in her situation the same. A transference of inner tranquillity and personal enrichment. Many of her friends benefitted from her change. And as others passed away around her she was able to console herself and console their families. A deep acceptance of how things are and how they will be.

In the coming years her wish was granted, and she passed away in the warmth and comfort of what close family and friends she had left. And to her immense relief, the Priest managed to find her at this time. There is little dignity in death but there can be in dying. She clung onto his arm as she breathed her last and then she smiled as her head gently fell back and her arm dropped. In the coming days both Imran and herself watched him lead her funeral prayers. They both joined in as he supplicated for her, sincerely and devoutly, acknowledging repeatedly "*Ameen, ameen, thumma ameen.*"

At this time she remembered the Priests parting words to her: "Dirt is always part of our lives. We are made from it, we walk over it and then we get covered by it." She had liked that. She liked it a lot.

# 18.  The Ephemeral Poet

"So, please start."

They were sitting on the floor in the Priest's lounge. Minimalist in decor although rich in ornamental accessories and punctuated with family history.  The Priest was sitting comfortably behind a small table that had an inclined reading surface and his student sat opposite, relaxed, quiet, attentive, but a little nervous.  It was mid-morning and the strong summer sun was beginning to shine through the tall bay windows at the end of the long lounge.  Outside was warm and humid.  Refreshing for those who were able to appreciate, too warm for those who could not.

The Priest had indicated to the student that he should begin his latest task.  It was unexpected as all the tasks were and his was not to question why, just to do and try.  However, he had questioned why he had to write poetry.  The answer he got was fascinating.

"In order to progress, you must have the heart of an explorer and the soul of a poet.  In this way strengths combine, weaknesses evaporate and a spiritual balance is achieved.  Our minds are divided into artistry and science.  Through their mergence do strong minds and souls make."

The student had been reflecting on his teachers comments. He realised that even in the military there are songs that are sung and music played.  The football terraces also have thousands of fans singing crude lyrics, competing with their opposite numbers in a sort of poetic challenge; encouraging their own teams and insulting their opponents. So song and poetry plays an interesting role in all lives, whether partaking or listening. Although to say that 'every moment is a moment of poetry' is a moment of vomiting.

So the student took a deep breath and began his first recitation.

"I fear...

All my sins and mistakes I do fear
Pleading and beseeching within a tear
The *musalla* overused, battered and worn
Hope from the heart viscously torn
I fear from misfortunes I do not benefit
Between good and bad too large a deficit
I fear my life before me, worthless
Blessings and rewards missed, priceless
I fear forgiveness sought is not gained
As hurt caused to others still remains
I fear reality just passing me by
Until my soul to heaven sighs
I fear mistakes good records nullify
Sincerity and intentions refusing to lie
I fear Ramadan rewards silently falling
Starving good deeds through false fasting
I fear the displeasure of my Creator
His mercy and kindness are needs of favour
I fear the shroud of cloth and dirt
When everything but deeds do desert

I fear the thin bridge over scorching flames
To cross or fall the question remains
I fear the book when presented
If left hand grasps it, then hopes be ended
I fear a future in the fire that rages
Its fuel of flesh and stone eternally blazes
I fear an existence without the most beloved
The greatest fear, hopes and dreams all blooded"

The student paused. He had begun the recitation with trepidation. As he got into the poem, he began to relax, settle and be himself inspired.

"Next," the Priest instructed. No comment or encouragement. Just 'next'.

So he again took a deep breath and recited his second piece.

"O nafs...

O nafs! I beg thee leave me alone
For all my sins I must and will atone
O nafs! You constantly whisper and you mislead
You deviate all, dealing pride and greed
O nafs! My *Iman* and *ihsan* you block and erode
But protection from the Mighty, *du'a* can bestow
O nafs! I know your help is devious, deceptive
My soul to protect and to guide, receptive
O nafs! your purpose to me and all is clear
Your whispers and falsehoods wise men fear
You confuse, misguide, and clarity muddle
We fight, we persevere, strive and struggle
O nafs! Despite my wishes your traits remain

Your influence ceases when life drains
O nafs! On that day, it will be clear and all will see
Who between us, be the final victory."

Again he paused, waiting for a comment or instructions.

"Next please," instructed the Priest.

The student looked up. A little concerned about his teachers abrupt comments. But the Priest was preparing him, toughening him up. His reaction to insult, criticism, lack of support, withholding of love, could not be one of upset or depression. He was destined to give and not to receive. He had to be a little brutal and merciless.

"There is...
There is a journey ahead ready to be started.
There is a darkness in your path ready to be illuminated.
There is a candle in your heart ready to be kindled.
There is a void in your soul ready to be filled.
There is a bridge in your life ready to be crossed.
There is a pain in your body ready to be soothed.
There is a light in your eyes ready to shine.
There is a beauty in your character ready to be seen.
There is a sound in your voice ready to be heard.
There is the purity of your intention ready to be rewarded.
There is a yearning within you ready to be satisfied.
There is a fire in your destiny ready to be extinguished.
There is error upon error ready to be forgiven.
There is a sadness in your look ready to be forgotten.
There is a hole in the ground ready to be filled.
There is a record of deeds ready to be judged.

There is the creator of creation there to be worshipped.
There is the greatest of creation destined to be loved."

"Is that it?" asked the Priest? "What about the *du'a* I asked
you for?

The student nodded. He indeed had written down the *du'a*
he had been asked to write. 'A summary of everything' he had
been asked to write. Maximum two sentences but preferably
one. So he prepared himself and took another breath.

"O Allah, you gave me emotion and capacity to love. So
allow me to love you and to love the one whom you love the
most. *Ameen.*"

"And?" asked the Priest. "The remainder please."

The student was surprised. He had written more but had no
intention of reading it as this was meant to be his own private
supplication. But he had been instructed.

"Replace my ignorance with knowledge
My folly with wisdom,
My weakness with strength
My impatience with fortitude
My despair with hope
My haste with patience
My darkness with light
My helplessness with steadfastness
My poverty with richness
My illness with health
My recklessness with prudence
My anger with serenity

My desires with nobility
My distress with happiness
My dreams with reality
My love with even more love
My problems with solutions
My tests with successes
My health with ever greater health
My tears with more tears
My sleep with worship
My emptiness with fulfilment
My laziness with devotion
My greed with satisfaction
My enemies with friends
My friendships with brotherhood
My failures with victories
My sadness with smiles
My pain with relief
My hunger with fasting
My joys with greater joys
My judgment with triumph
My final breath with *kalimah tayyibah*
My jahannum with jannah
And my all for company with your beloved."

The Priest listened quietly, and then instructed, "And the last one?"

The student took another deep breath. Again, his personal and private contemplations were about to be read out. Not what he had in mind.

"Denying the existence of Allah is denying our own existence.
Denying Islam as *Haqq* is denying the truth within us and around us.
Denying the Holy Qur'an is denying our salvation.
Denying our beloved Prophet Muhammad (ﷺ) is denying the entire creation."

There was a long silence. The Priest was reflecting on the poetry. He then starting asking the student questions. The student was amazed at the Priest's memory. He asked him questions quoting verbatim lines from each poem, while he himself had to read off his sheets of paper. This was a revelation. The student knew the Priest had a powerful intellect and impressive mind, but not this powerful. He doubted anyone else knew this fact while he attempted to answer his beloved teacher's questions. For around fifteen minutes the intense and probing discussion continued. Then a welcome respite.

There had now been silence in the room for about five minutes. Hearts were beating rhythmically, minds were working serenely, breaths were being taken calmly. The Priest then shifted his body a little and opened his mouth to speak.

"*Alhamdulillah*," he said. "That's all for today. Will see you next week *inshaAllah*."

And that was it.

# 19.   Inner Peace.

The discussion was in full swing. The Priest was speaking to a hard-line secularist. An evolutionist fan who believed madly in secularism and was able to argue the case against religion extremely well. He had heard about this Priest and thought he would score another notch on his victory chart. This was basically a picture of a monkey with carefully placed victory lines along the bottom of the poster with every four vertical lines crossed to make a five. Twenty seven was his number so far. Not a single defeat. So it had started. The twenty eighth battle.

"You can't see God, you can't show me God, you can't even prove God," the young man again repeated for the third time. Most recognised scientists don't believe for these reasons."

"But what's that got to do with evolution?" asked the Priest. "The fact that most Noble prize winners are not believers or from the Muslim world?"

The discussion had bounced around a bit as the evolutionist was using all of his arguments to prevent himself struggling. And struggling he was. He had stated that so few Muslims had won the Nobel prize worked in favour of his standpoint.

"Well it shows that the religion is wrong," argued the young man.

"Actually, it shows that the opposite is true," corrected the Priest.

"How?"

It was nearing the end of summer. Still warm and pleasant but beginning to cool. In the Priest's small office a special meeting had been arranged with this secularist. He had trolled the internet and debated with those brave enough to face him. He was also recording this for his web page to show all his followers yet another defeated religious person. He was in his early thirties, fair, dark hair with a strange haircut and a cheap, black plastic earring. His hair appeared to have been dyed in faint streaks along his sides by his ears. Subtle and weird. It looked like he had visited a schizophrenic barber. However, it bought him attention and created an image which is what he wanted.

The Priest answered his question. "Because," he began, "if most Nobel prize winners believe in God and if Nobel prizes are your guide then belief in God is the right thing. And if I can show you that most of them do, then?"

The young man paused for thought. Yes that's true he thought. "But you need to show me," He said as he adjusted his cheap plastic black earring on his left ear-lobe.

"Of course," responded the Priest. "Also," he continued "the fact that the Muslim world gave civilisation its civilisation also shows that belief in God creates intellectual and technical advancement. We've already discussed Algebra, Chemistry, Arabic numerals, eye surgery, universities, libraries...all founded by great Muslim scholars of the past. Even things like empirical assessment, the water cycle, piston engines, time keeping and the number 'zero' are all discoveries and inventions of these scientists. So Nobel prize-wise and civilisation wise, belief in God is key."

"But most scientists don't believe in God and look how the world is advancing," asked the young man, using normally one of his decisive arguments. This time though he was not as confident.

"You see," the Priest began, I believe most scientists believe in some sort of higher power but many are scared or too arrogant to admit it. But they can't deny the evidence that they themselves have discovered. One can't help but ask the questions, 'is there nothing more?' 'Is this all that I am?' You honestly don't believe there is nothing after death do you?"

A silence. This discussion was not going as planned and neither was it going anywhere useful. Now he had been asked a direct question which he needed to answer. He decided to use his practiced tactic of answering it with another question.

"Well, there is no proof of life after death is there. I mean you can't really prove it. No one can."

The Priest sat back a little in his chair and closed his eyes for a second or so. Coffee and biscuits had been consumed a long time ago. He had work to do, but this was also his work and he decided to lead the discussion to a close.

"There are three clear and convincing proofs," began the Priest. "And I would like you to consider them carefully."

At this point, the young man's brain sent a signal to his adrenal glands to pump a little adrenalin into his system. Three proofs? This he would like to hear. He was on alert and forgot about his earring for a second.

"The first is in the study of physics," explained the Priest. The concept of dimensions is clearly accepted by all the scientific community, whether they believe in God or not. Ten dimensions have been proposed by some. These are known about, but unseen. Theory predicts them but they cannot be experienced. So no-one can deny that this could be an aspect of life after death. It is not a wormhole that transports a person to a different dimension or to another universe, it could just as well be death. It could also just as well be conception which transports us into this dimension which we know."

"But that's just speculation," objected the young man.

"It is as feasible a speculation as not believing in it," responded the Priest immediately. "And then there is the second proof. If God does exist, then he would have wished us to be guided and informed about himself as well as the afterlife. After all, these are fundamental beliefs. In our scriptures, we have evidence of there being 124,000 prophets who have come to explain this. To be perfectly frank, the current world just needs one last one, and in fact it only remembers a few. We cannot deny our human history – Moses, Abraham, Noah, Isac, Jesus and Prophet Muhammad, peace be upon them all. All humanity believes they existed, thus it follows that there is a truth here; a common truth and a persistent thread in our beliefs and our consciences. All preached and informed us about life after death, and there is no denying this. It is a common message amongst all main beliefs."

The young man was quietly listening.

"And the final proof is the strongest of all," said the Priest a little more quietly. "It is as clear as it is profound and powerful. It is the proof within yourself. You cannot deny your heart telling you that death is not the end. You cannot silence it no matter how much you argue with yourself. You cannot see yourself in your grave – cremated or not – and possibly imagine that you are no more. Is your life really that worthless? Is this discussion that pointless? Is our special nature, our world, our universe made for no reason whatsoever? Is this just meaningless play and amusement? Surely such an unimaginative and weak conclusion is derogatory to our own intellect and existence. We have a pride in our existence, in our hopes and aspirations, in our accomplishments and in our good deeds. And then we say it's all pointless? Worthless? Hopeless? Really?"

A pause as the Priest sat back a little more and relaxed. His body language indicating that he had completed this part of the discussion and was inviting a comment.

"But," responded the young man, "the scientific community does not accept this. They cannot all be wrong?"

"No," responded the Priest. I believe most scientists do accept the creation of man by God until they find more direct evidence of definitive proof of evolution from animals to humans. Evolution cannot explain the chasm that exists between the two species – humans and animals. At all levels of intellect, consciousness and creed. The one who believes he was evolved from an animal, deserves to believe it and be called so." He paused as he gathered some more thoughts together. "This is a massive, huge missing link that no theory can explain, except the only logical theory, which concerns and requires divinity. After all... do you sincerely believe that your great, great grandfather was a monkey? Is that where you firmly believe you are from?"

Then, both engrossed participants were brought back to the real world as a car skidded outside. They both involuntarily glanced out of the window as the small, pathetic hatchback quickly sped away with its young driver having tried a handbrake turn and failed. The Priest then breathed in deeply and out calmly and slowly before he continued.

"We cannot deny history. We cannot deny our hearts. We cannot deny our souls. We cannot deny the evidence all around us and the lack of evidence all around us. We pride ourselves as living in a progressive society, one with heightened levels of intellect and ability. But we are so arrogant, that we do deny reality."

The young man was staring directly at the Priest's eyes. He was taking as much in as he could. After a short pause, he then changed the direction of the discussion to the big bang as in his mind, physics and astronomy had been able to show once and for all that there was no 'great power' involved in its occurrence.

"We have shown," he began slowly, "that the entire universe functions and sustains itself. There is no God in this equation. Everything has been proven and explained and those things that are left will also be explained. We know in detail what happened during the big bang until today and also what is going to happen in the infinite future. The universe doesn't need any God."

The Priest listened patiently to the well rehearsed sentence. However, rather than answer it how the young man expected, he decided to include latest scientific knowledge on the nature of the universe.

"That's really very interesting," said the Priest. "I would say that the energy in the universe didn't just come from no-where, it came from somewhere. The laws governing it also haven't just appeared, they have been placed there. And there are many things we know about but we can never understand them except through difficult theory and difficult empirical measurement. Even then, we will never be sure."

"Like what?" the young man asked. He was perturbed as his happiness and contentment of his position rested heavily on this scientific basis. "Some examples please of things we can never know about."

"Well," explained the Priest, "for example, black holes, dark matter, dark energy what happened before the creation of time and different dimensions to name but a few. Can we go to a black hole to find out about it? Other dimensions? Has anyone seen any dark mater or dark energy? These things are beyond us as they defy our perceptions and hide from our science."

There was a quiet, reflective silence for a short time as both participants pondered.

"But there is always theory," insisted the young man.

"Yes," responded the Priest. "Theory will always remain theory. We had to go to the moon before realising where it came from. But we can't travel back in time or into a black hole or into the future or to different dimensions or put some dark energy into a test tube. No. In fact, 99% of the universe is hidden to us and hidden to our understanding of it. 99% is dark matter and dark energy. Dark matter travels through normal matter and doesn't reflect or emit light but it holds normal matter together. Amazing but true. As only a small amount of the universe actually is normal matter, most of the universe is not just unseeable but also unknowable to us, and unknown to scientists, no matter how many prizes they win."

Now an informed silence. No matter what he has said before the young man knew this to be true. Most of the universe is dark to us, i.e. invisible. We can't actually see it or realise it or even experience it. 'Incredible but true,' he thought.

"But that doesn't prove God though does it?" he asked a little nervously now as his mind struggled to keep up with the discussion. Or rather with the lesson.

"The universe is so dark," continued the Priest, ignoring the question for time being, Astronomers didn't even know that there was a super-massive black hole at the centre of practically every Galaxy. How could you miss what you later call 'super-massive'? Anyway, coming to your question, it does prove God's existence and it proves it in a number of ways. Only a supreme power can explain the logic and reality of what we see and what we don't see. Only such power can explain the huge amount of energy in this universe. Only such a power can explicate the fact that the existence of colourful and beautiful life in this dark universe defies all logic and reason. The mere knowing we exist cannot hide the fact that we exist in such a vast, dark cosmos full of dangers and uncertainty and also the fact that all probability is against the development of life. We have to accept there is dark matter and dark energy and that they make up the majority of what we see and cannot see. So why is it too much to ask for belief in the Creator for such beauty and wonder, whom we also cannot see? While the proof of his creation is everywhere."

The young man listened and made the connection as he began to nod, to his surprise. He then stopped nodding immediately.

"We live in the shadows. We are insignificant, and now we have to believe that most of what exists we can't see and never will. Science has done a full circle. It always argued to believe in what you can see and experiment with. Now it is saying believe in what you cannot see. Trust us that it is there – different dimensions, dark matter and dark energy but we can't see them and we can't show them to you and we can't even prove it. 99%! Haven't we heard these arguments before?"

'Yes', thought the young man. He had heard them before.

"The message of science now, is very similar to the message of all 124,000 prophets. To believe in the unseen and unknown. The true unification theory, leading to the only one possible conclusion."

And so the discussion began to gradually end. Just a few repeats of the same thing, then polite small-talk remained and eventually the goodbyes.

For the young man with the weird hair and cheap earring, he was contemplating the meeting and the discussion. His mind was consciously and subconsciously assessing and appreciating the knowledge discussed, debated and shared. The last few words were still ringing in the young man's head: "A progressive society is not one that turns its backs on truth and authentic scripture; but it is one that embraces it. Even our own arrogance cannot grant us more knowledge than the creator of all knowledge."

"Deep," thought the young man, "deep," as he adjusted his cheap earring.

# 20. *Quotes and Clichés*

It was quite an amusing scene. The taxi driver was trying to impress his passenger, who happened to be the Spirit Priest. On this occasion it was his extensive memory of quotes and clichés. He had developed this since he was a child, making use of his photographic memory. He used this quality to try to keep his passengers amused and at the same time to test himself. After all, taxi driving was very boring, repetitive and lonely.

The Priest was sitting quietly at the back, resting after a full eleven hours of counselling. He must have seen almost 40 families and was on his way to another family's house who had requested him to stay with them.

The taxi was proceeding along the quiet streets of Manchester. It was dry, dark and warm. The air conditioning of the vehicle provided a refreshing breeze and the cheap, scented, tree hanging off the dashboard oozing the traditional taxi cologne.

"I could speak in clichés until the cows come home," remarked the taxi driver. "So why don't you test me and see how many anecdotes, quotes and clichés I know?" he asked.

The Priest was tired, but this interested him. "I tell you what," the Priest replied, "I agree, except you must only tell me inspiring quotes, ones which have good lessons for us."

The taxi driver became interested all of a sudden, more than normal. "I accept," he said. "It's a good challenge."

"So I'm listening," said the Priest. "Please continue."

"Okay," said the taxi driver. "You won't be disappointed. Let me just scan my mental field and choose the correct ones." For the next few seconds his photographic brain went into search mode and he mentally flew over his stored fields of pictures, words and images. He chose the correct one and then populated it with the relevant images, creating a story-board which he now began to read out.

"Said a wise student: 'Knowledge is like a tool. It stays useful if you use it, otherwise it will rust.' "

His voice had changed slightly to become a bit more dramatic and preacher like. With a perfect pause between each of his quotes.

"Said a wise teacher: 'The best knowledge is that expressed through action and the weakest through speech.'

Said an unfit, trainee swimmer: 'My best for the 100m is 80m.'

Said a gifted student: 'If you tell me I will listen, if you show me I will learn and if you involve me, I will understand.'

Said a sage: 'It is better to correct the true self rather than hide behind a mask.'

Said the England Football Manager: 'I have chosen my team to win the next world cup. It's Brazil.'

Said a saint: 'The problem with the world is that intelligent people are full of doubt and the ignorant are full of confidence.'

Said a sagacious leader: 'Try your best to be both soft and strong as that is a combination very few have mastered. Being soft wins hearts and being strong helps to protect your own.'

Said a proud gardener: 'I have 500 people working under me. That's because I cut the grass at a cemetery.'

Said a rejected love: 'Appreciate those who love ya. Help those who need ya. Forgive those who hurt ya. Forget those who leave ya.' "

A horn suddenly blazed behind them. It was not directed at the Taxi (which was unusual for Manchester), but at some pedestrians whose attention the young driver and his mate managed to obtain. Childish shouts, giggles and screams then ensued. The Taxi driver then continued his presentation.

"Said a lonely tramp: 'This world is like a snake, soft to touch, but full of venom inside.'

Said a hurting individual: 'Friends come and go. Enemies accumulate.'

Said a wealthy and sick person: 'I give in charity as I need the reward more than the beggar needs the money.'

Said a happy husband to his wife: 'I just swatted 5 flies in the kitchen - two males and 3 females'. His wife asked him how he knew. To which he replied, 'two were on the pizza and three the phone.'

Said a policeman: 'The murdered man was deaf, dumb and blind. It was a senseless killing.'

Said an old and lonely person: 'Generosity is when you help a needy person without their request.'

He paused his recitation and then asked, "How am I doing? Are these the sayings you are looking for?"

The Priest was tired but refreshed with these expressions of knowledge, humour and wisdom. It was proving to be a very pleasant experience. "Yes," he said in reply to the question. "They are all very inspiring. Please do continue."

So urged on and much happier, he continued as the taxi bumped along the quiet roads.

"Said a divorcee: 'A relationship without trust is like a car without an engine. You can stay in it as long as you wish but it won't go anywhere.'

Said an unemployed man: 'If you find silliness with you, try and leave it behind, otherwise it will stay with you wherever you go.'

Said a window cleaner: 'Never step back to admire your work.'

Said a wise fisherman: 'Never test the depth of water with both feet.'

Said a professor: 'Speech is a scale which reason makes weighty, ignorance makes weightless, wisdom makes useful, softness makes accepted.'

Said a curious student: 'I stopped asking so many questions, then finally started hearing the answers.'

Said a farmer: 'The easiest type of farming is wind farming.'

Said a kung fu master: 'The one who lives in the past, he deprives his present, the one who does not learn from his past he deprives his future.'

Said a distraught monk: 'Even if a mirror is broken into a thousand pieces, there will still be a thousand reflections. We should reflect on this world in a thousand ways. Enemies reflect your faults, friends reflect your qualities, and teachers reflect your potential.' "

The taxi now stopped at a red light. Some happy drunk youths crossed the road, trying to keep each other upright, enjoying their drunkard, ignorant bliss. One had vomited down the front of his football T shirt and appeared to be enjoying that bliss as well. The lights turned green and the taxi continued on its way as did the driver.

"Said a Doctor: 'An intelligent person lowers himself to attain a high status while a foolish person raises his status thereby disgracing himself.'

Said a Sufi: 'You cannot give anything to your ego, except indifference.'

Said a philosopher: 'A wise enemy is better than a foolish friend.'

Said an army General: 'War does not determine who is right. It simply determines who is left standing.'

Said a guidance councillor: 'Marriage is not about whom you can live with. It's about whom you cannot live without.'

Said a failed Politician: 'The world is a strange place where those that lack modesty are considered beautiful, cheaters are considered clever, and the loyal are considered foolish.'

Said a superhero: 'Sometimes the good you do doesn't do you any good.'

Said an upset daughter: 'The problem with common sense is that it is not very common.'

Said a judge: 'You have been shown, if you only care to see; you have been advised if you care to take advantage of it; you have been told if you care to listen.'

Said a weatherman: 'Pollen count is a difficult job.'

Said a Sufi scholar: 'It's not what you look at but what you see that counts. It's not what you hear, but what you listen to that matters. It's not what you say, but what you mean that's important. It's not what you think, but what you ponder over that inspires.'

Narrated a top Sifu: 'The highest art is to hit a person such that he doesn't know who hit him.'

Said a wise man: 'I never lost an argument with a knowledgeable person but I lost all my arguments with an ignorant person.' "

The driver suddenly had to slow down as a van decided to pull out right in front of him. He was multitasking well. A safe driver, even though his mind was occupied elsewhere. He only paused for a few seconds as the van performed a full U-turn and then without any derogatory comment (unusual for

Manchester), he simply continued to drive. The entire incident was completely un-dramatic as if it had been rehearsed. He was a certainly a mature driver. He then continued his recital as if he had not even paused.

"Said an Indian Apache: 'The man who chase after two buffalo catches none.'

Said a taxi driver after he crashed into a lemon tree: 'I'm still bitter and twisted.'

Said a senior Mafia man: 'The lion is silent but feared. The dog barks but is chased off.'

Said a professor of life: 'True intelligence is when you learn from all around you.'

Said a Teacher who lost his Thesaurus: 'I can't find the words to express my sadness.'

Narrated a wise Geologist: 'A diamond is a lump of coal that has handled stress really well.'

Explained a President: 'I said whatever I needed to in order to get power, and I will do whatever I need to in order to stay in power.'

Said a sage: 'Knowledge without action is hypocrisy and action without knowledge is ignorance.'

Said an inspired philosopher: 'We should be like a seed. If it is dropped into dirt and covered in darkness - it struggles to reach the light.'

When asked by a salesman if he required an alternative energy source, the householder answered: 'No, I'm happy with electricity and gas.'

Said a hen-pecked husband: 'The best speech is if you say little but your few words mean lot.'

Said a failed monk: 'You can't conquer the world with goodness, but you can conquer it with truth.'

Said Superman: 'Kryptonite is a pain in the neck. It was only invented to make me vincible.'

Said an old man: 'Live life like a pair of walking feet, the foot that is forward has no pride and the foot behind has no shame. This is because they both know their situation will change'

Said a humorous physicist: 'Don't trust atoms, they make up everything.'

Explained a dietician: 'We can see the effects of dieting with this pie chart.'

Explained a Shaolin Master: 'This art is not *self-defence*, but *opponent attack*.'

Said a defeated politician: 'Pride is concerned with whom is right. Humility is concerned with what is right.'

Said a psychiatrist: 'females can hide their love for 40 years but cannot hide hatred even for a single hour.'

Said a financier: 'Give a man a gun and he can rob a bank. Give a man a bank and he can rob the world.'

Said a Priest: 'A man is either your brother in faith or your brother in humanity.'

Asked a wife to her husband: 'Is there anything on the TV?' 'Dust', replied the husband. Then the fight started...

My wife was hinting about what she wanted for our upcoming Anniversary. She said, 'I want something shiny that goes from 0 to 150 in about 3 seconds.' I bought her a set of scales. Then the fight started...

A woman is standing looking in the bedroom mirror. She is not happy with what she sees and says to her husband, 'I feel Horrible; I look old, fat and ugly. I really need you to pay me a Compliment.' The husband replies, 'Your eyesight's perfect.' Then the fight started...

The journey was now over. The Priest disembarked, paid the driver, and his parting words to him were thus: "The body is purified by water, ego by tears, intellect by knowledge, the soul by love and friendship with humour. God bless you for spreading all of these to those whom you meet."

The Priest left and quickly walked out of sight. The driver instantly learned the Priest's quote and then extrapolated several other deep spiritual quotes as if inspired. He never saw the Priest again, and although he had done almost all the talking, he felt he had learned the most.

# 21.  The Sajdah

The mother was sobbing in-front of the Priest.  Even now she had not come to terms with what had happened and what her son had done.  She was traditionally dressed in a *shalwar kameez* and loose fitting *dupatta*.  The entire family and the whole community were in a state of shock as a result of what had transpired.

"I'm all alone," she cried.  "I've failed... I've raised a monster.  It's all so horrible and I can't believe it.  I don't know what to do, where to go.  I can't show my face anywhere."

The story was simple but it was disturbing to the core.  Unspeakable evil in plain view, rather than hidden in the darkness as all would prefer.  It concerned her son.  In one sense, a young, typical teenager with bad company and drugs.  In another sense, someone totally inhuman.

It was a traumatic time for the boy.  He had been slapped repeatedly by his father and shouted at by his mum.  He had been caught stealing money and using it to feed his habit.  Taking weed now daily and staying away from home for long periods.  They had had enough.  His mum's jewellery stolen, his father's debit card taken, and his account emptied.  If there was ever a time for a telling off, it was now.  The parents were lost and distraught.  Mother was in tears and the father uncontrollably angry.  They had now hidden all the jewellery, cards and cash and their son – the boy – was demanding money or he would start destroying the house.  He then attacked his dad - hence the slap and the shouting.  He was now quiet but fuming. His father, meanwhile decided to go to his local Imam to seek advice as well as to calm himself down and try and understand what had occurred. This was not supposed to happen.

In another sense he was not the typical teenager. No tattoos, no earrings, no bling. Nothing to show his destructive character and what lurked within. He had lied so much that he was now a professional swindler. Well kept hair, slim physique, designer clothes (well, cheap, foreign rip-offs) and a ridiculously large watch, almost large enough for a wall. A pleasant five foot seven inches tall and a sweet, charming voice. No stereotyping possible with his innocent looks and youthful charm. A really nice, trustworthy person on the outside, destructive and evil on the inside.

The father arrived at the Mosque at prayer time so was not able to obtain guidance from the Imam straight away. He simply joined in the prayers in the back row. Meanwhile the boy was experiencing more frustration and anger from his mother for which he kept quiet. What no-one realised was that he was still on a high and despite that he had a soft spot for his mum so he didn't answer back. His father, however, was another matter. He was totally against him and quietly fuming. So the boy decided to complete an action he had been contemplating for a few weeks. Enough was enough. He went upstairs and searched under his mattress. He had cut a small incision into it and hidden a jagged knife in a sheath which he had bought months before. He had showed it once to a drug dealer when he was being overcharged but other than that had kept it for protection in this dangerous world of highs. It was not a small knife. It had a curved handle made of heavy duty, black plastic and a sharpened, toughened, jagged blade continuing the curvature to a sharp point. Its use determined its design – elegant, efficient and deadly. It looked fit for purpose.

The knife was housed in a sheath which could be attached to the side of a person's shin, hidden under a trouser leg. But the boy chose to put it in his pocket. After all, 'this won't take long,' he thought.

He left the house in full view of his mother and obviously she was not able to stop him, still in tears and still complaining her frustrations. He hurried out of his front door and headed towards the Mosque. 'The sooner this is over, the better,' he thought. His heart was racing and his head was hurting. 'I must do this,' he kept saying to himself 'in-front of everyone.' The words were powerful, compelling and persistent. He had no choice, no strength to resist. His mission must be successful. An irresistible urge to do something horrific. This had been repeated to him again and again and again until he was worn down and powerless. This way he would gain some peace, some closure, some relief. Thus the mission was set and the race to fulfil it had begun. It had to be done and had to be done quickly, decisively and without compassion and without thought.

No one could see this silent whisperer, playing on the boys mind and then this boy adopting this evil. Not evil within him but evil grafted and grafted well. A constant urging, continuous talking, an incessant bombardment of words in his head. Refusing to stop unless they were actioned.

So he entered the Mosque but did not take his shoes off. He heard the *takbir* as he walked into the prayer hall. He found everyone in *sajdah*. The worshippers then came out of *sajdah* as he tried to locate his worst enemy - his father. He spotted him in the last line towards his left. His hand now grabbed his knife in a determined and powerful way. He unsheathed it as he hurried towards his father while the Imam again pronounced the *takbir* and the worshippers went into *sajdah* for the second time. He positioned himself between his father and the next worshipper and then without hesitation, he held his father head by his hair to keep it on the ground with one hand, and performed the deed with the knife in the other hand.

The unthinkable. The unimaginable. The incomprehensible. The utterly horrific and horrendous. What unspeakable things are rehearsed in someone's mind and then are acted out in the real world. This most horrific evil took just a few seconds. A gentle motion of the knife – brief and quiet. A short nightmare but with a lifetime of consequences. The boy stepped back as his father just collapsed and turned over. Their eyes met briefly. His father's were full of shock, confusion and disbelief. The boys eyes were wide, and were icy, piercing and vengeful. Stone cold and devoid of any emotion save intense anger.

Then the boy turned and ran. His father's fellow worshippers now realised. They broke their prayer and tried to stop the blood from flowing out of the massive gash in his neck. It wouldn't work. A commotion as the blood just gushed out from between their fingers. The blood was fresh and it was warm and it was chilling. The father with a look of utter helplessness on his face as he frantically tried to grab his neck and stop the blood. But he quickly fell unconscious whilst his heart continued to pump. His body going limp and lifeless. Worshippers now started shouting and screaming for an ambulance, knowing that it was quite hopeless as they witnessed the last few moments of someone's life. Mobile phones calling 999. This man was dying and he was dying fast. It was real but it was not. The bright red life-giving liquid now effortlessly and rapidly draining life. Flowing out thick and flowing out fast. An unholy, ugly stain, soaking the sacred carpet and growing with every heart-beat.

The boy had long since gone. The bloodied knife safely sheathed and back in his pocket. He was going to calmly catch a tube and travel to his friends who were fellow takers of drugs. A really nice, trustworthy person on the outside. Full of turmoil, upset, anger and addiction on the inside. And now he had graduated to becoming a murderer on the outside. A bitter, unforgiving and murderous teenager – the inevitable product of this immoral, civilised world.

The mother was till sobbing in front of the Priest. Her husband's funeral had just occurred a few weeks ago. The Priest was quiet; listening; thinking. Her son had been caught. Unremorseful and unrepentant. A juvenile. The state had no tools or ways to deal with him; only to lock him away and blame his mental state.

They had not seen the Priest at all before this. Now they saw him to obtain guidance in their darkness and their upset. To obtain answers from questions that no one else could answer; to lead them through this emptiness; to bring some meaning back, some hope, some answers.

They say that a time will come when the murdered is asked why? And he has no answer. And the murderer is asked why? And he also has no answer. That time is here and that time is now.

The Priest did not provide many answers, except one. And this he kept to himself. The demon world had once again reared its ugly head.

# 22.   The Theme Park

"So can you help?" asked the Detective. "Could you help us do you think?"

It was late summer and unusually hot. The pleasant warm air and glorious sunshine contrasting with the dark, dreary and devilish deeds. The policeman was sitting in the Priest's office. His focus was on the case he had been assigned. A young girl abducted from his local area and no real witnesses. He had approached the Priest a few days before and had been following his direction as to where to look and search. He had turned up blank, so was back.

There was a little boy who apparently had seen a young girl 'walking towards a wooded area' at the edge of town. She wasn't far from her home. Her parents had let her go with her friends to walk and talk. Unknown to them, the kids had a falling out in the park and separated. Then nothing. Dogs, police, volunteers, all found nothing after days of searching.

The Priest had asked for specifics, including that information not in newspapers. He had been told everything the police had, even though it was against regulations. The Detective trusted him and was desperate to find her. She had been missing for five days now and the Priest had agreed to help on condition that he was not mentioned.

"We found one clue," disclosed the Detective, "where you asked us to look. Near the little brook. There were footprints but nothing definite. They could have been made by anyone."

"Did you take any photographs?" asked the Priest.

"Yes," he responded as the Detective rummaged for his large screen Smartphone. He was well presented with silver cuffs on a well-ironed crease-free shirt with a cool, open top button. His trousers were well pressed. He took it out of his pocket He was energetic, eager and focused as this was his first proper case. Too much social work in Policing, so he was eager for some crime solving cases. He had landed a serious one.

The family of the young girl were distraught. She was the younger of two siblings and had just turned 12. They had trusted her friends to look after her, one of them being her cousin. Now they were in this awful position where their daughter's condition or whereabouts were totally unknown. They had been living their lives with the normal assumptions of safety, eternity and the fact that anything bad or evil happens to others and not to them. Their perpetual theme park, now brought crashing down around them.

The Police had hinted that the longer it took, then they may need to prepare for the worst. But the Priest had given the Detective some hope. He had told him that there was a chance she was still alive. So he was filled with a greater urge to find her.

"Can you enlarge the picture please?" asked the Priest as he was handed a small marvel in electronic engineering. With this device one can connect to the world and anyone in the world, with Apps for virtually everything. However, one can't find a lost person, so not good enough really – not that 'smart'.

"Do you see?" asked the Priest. He was pointing at the enlarged picture, where clearly there were many footprints.

"Yes," said the Detective. "But we checked all these. They were a real mixture and looked like they had been there for ages."

"No," replied the Priest. "Look." He was pointing to a deep indentation in the ground. "This is where someone struggled to pick her up."

"Pick who up?" asked the Detective.

"Pick up the little girl," he responded. "He struggled as she resisted, so he ended up on one leg and had to dig his foot into the soft mud, hence the indentation. And look at this," as he pointed out some more areas. "This is where she was sitting throwing stones into the brook. And I believe the kidnapper came up behind her and grabbed her and put his hand over her mouth to muffle her screams before he scared her to keep quiet. As it was near dusk, there was no-one else around and he knew that."

This was too much for the Detective now. He had to ask. "So is she still alive?"

The Priest paused and was staring into the distance. "Possibly," he replied. "But we need to find her quickly. You need to look for someone who visits that place at weekends. He's a loner. Quiet, simple and likes the outdoors. People have seen him there."

"Yes," responded the Detective, "but we have asked everyone already."

"I know," agreed the Priest, "he may even have already been interviewed, but you have ruled him out and you haven't checked out his alibi. He probably said he was at home and there the day before or the week before or something like that. He can't live too far. A few miles. I hope he hasn't killed her yet but he will do."

"Why is he holding her?" asked the Detective.

"Please," replied the Priest, "you know. We both know."

"So," began the Detective. "Where do we look?"

"You must ask around for a van or four-wheel drive vehicle," responded the Priest.

"But please tell me where she is?" pleaded the Detective.

"Probably in his house," replied the Priest. "I don't think you have very long."

So the Detective once again started making enquiries, door to door. Even though it was the weekend, he was upset, angry and determined. He had gone through his notes and others' notes but could not link any interview undertaken with anyone who had a four-wheel drive. There were just names and addresses. So it was back to traditional police work, canvassing face to face. Lots of open questions to try and jog people's memories – but no memories to jog. He also roamed the woods hoping to catch this elusive person or speak to someone who may have seen him. But nothing – a complete blank. It was frustrating and appeared hopeless. Then a brainwave.

"So do you remember anything?" the Detective asked the attendant for the second time.

This was the third petrol station the Detective had visited. It was getting late and he was exhausted. Detectives are trained not to undertake critical tasks when overly tired, but this was guidance rarely followed, especially at times like this.

The petrol attendant was busy serving customers, but that was in his automatic mode, while his brain was thinking about the question. "I do," he replied, and continued thinking as the customer completed her transaction and a second took her place. "It was a white 4x4" he declared. "Yes. He came in maybe last week or week before and the reason I remember him is that he was in combat trousers. But I haven't seen him since. He comes in every few weeks or months; goes camping and the like I think."

The Detective started to get a little more interested. "You don't happen to remember the registration or make of the car?" he asked.

The attendant started to shake his head as he continued to serve. "No, sorry," he replied. "It was a foreign 4x4, darkened windows, but no, no registration."

"What about the cameras?" asked the Detective. "They must have picked him up."

"No, sorry," replied the attendant again, "they haven't worked all month. Hopefully next week they will be fixed."

Again, another disappointment after he had appeared to make some progress. Now a dead end. The Detective then asked for a description or name, but also drew a blank as all he remembered was the vehicle and the fatigues. So he quietly watched him serve the final customer who quickly paid and left the petrol station. The Detective still stood there patiently as he saw the Asian attendant still thinking. He hoped for more useful information and his patience was rewarded.

"There was one thing," the attendant said. His face was focused as his memories tried to recount scenes from the monotonous and mundane. "The last time he was here he bought some cuddly toy and sweets."

"When was this?" asked the Detective.

"It was a last week and it was late."

Then the Detective asked the question he had been reserving but now was the time he had to ask. "Was it around the time that the young girl disappeared?"

A pause. A short one and a traumatic one. The Detective held his breath as he waited for the answer.

"Hmmm," as the attendant let out a thoughtful precursor to his next words. "Maybe," he said. Then a little more thought as the Detective still held his breath. "Yes," he replied, "I do believe it was that day or one day before or afterwards. Yes."

The Detectives mind was now working in overdrive (and he breathed out). The mechanics and motives of this crime would work whichever day it was, before the kidnapping, on the day of it, or even after. Before meant he had been planning it. On the same day means that the girl could have been tied up and gagged in his vehicle whilst in the petrol station. The day after means he required some supplies for the young girl but that was less likely as it meant returning to the scene of the crime.

More plausible was that it was an opportunist kidnapping by a closet paedophile. A product of a civilised, free world. Freedom to do whatever one likes between consenting adults. This does not harm any one person per se, but indeed endangers our entire society. When one immoral act becomes legalised, a path towards greater immorality also becomes legalised. Such a direction can be tremendously seductive. It creates a huge dissatisfaction in oneself and an insatiable desire for greater and greater gratification. Such a craving can never be fulfilled but it is always anticipated that contentment can be found at the next level. And now we are at one of those levels. A kidnapped girl. Another victim of an arrogant, ignorant and liberated society. Liberated from decency and void of the most essential and basic morality. A brutal, ugly truth, ignored at our peril. Evil cannot easily be recognised as a person becomes a human being by virtue of character, not by appearance.

So far the Priest had been accurate. Now a Police artist had been summoned to draw whatever he could from the memories of this young pump attendant. He indeed produced something, although not too much like the perpetrator. No distinguishing marks, no peculiar features, just a normal, nice guy. Outwardly standard but inwardly dirty. A diseased heart and an ugly, toxic soul.

So the search was on. Now the working week had started, more officers were involved searching the databases for a white 4x4 in the area within a fifty mile radius. Over forty were found. Each was traced and would be investigated that day if possible. Unfortunately all of the owners found so far had no possible connection to this crime for various reasons, one being the darkened windows for example. Even though there were a few left to enquire about, the Detective had a question. What if it had been re-sprayed and wasn't white to begin with? Then it could become a much more significant search, vast and complicated. However, this was their only concrete lead. Forensics at the crime scene had found tracks of car tyres but when the Priest had been consulted, he had advised it was very likely that the 4x4 had new, cheap tyres fitted, possibly part-worn.

The second day of the week and still nothing. As there were no new leads, the Detective decided to follow some up himself to speed up the process. One person stood out as he scanned the list of owners. A small village in Surrey, but the person had changed his name in previous years. Nothing on the database though for his previous name. But then police forces across different regions were not sharing data so he had to put an emergency request in for information. The Detective saw that this person was scheduled to be visited the next day but he decided to investigate himself. He drove down to the suspects address but called the Priest before leaving, asking for his blessing. The Detective had not been trained for firearms so felt a little vulnerable. However, he had informed his local commander of his trip. He just couldn't sit and do nothing. The Priest had advised him to go with someone, and the Detective assured him that he would. But there was no-one available and he felt a huge urge to investigate.

The journey was fine, not too much traffic. His sat-nav led him to a row of houses in a typical affluent village street. All had double garages and all detached on a quiet side road with pleasant woods on three sides. No 4x4 vehicle to be seen anywhere. He parked at the beginning of the street and proceeded to get out of the car. An Asian-faced Detective would be a curiosity in an all white village so he did get some interesting looks from those who happened to be out on this warm summer morning. The sun was shining behind clear, blue skies. The Detective felt fresh and crisp as he walked calmly to the address listed. His adrenalin was pumping and his newly dry-cleaned shirt and trousers fit nicely onto his slim and toned build. Hi aftershave wafting pleasantly. He pressed the bell which appeared not to work so knocked on the door with his knuckles, his ID ready to be shown. No answer. He knocked again but still no answer. After a minute he went next door and pressed the bell for attention. Within a few seconds a fresh-faced old gentleman slowly answered the door with a permanent smile on his face. Extremely refreshing considering the circumstances. He must have been watching curiously as quiet neighbours tend to do.

"Nothing to worry about sir, I'm a Detective working for the Police," as he flashed his ID.

"How may I help you young man?" he asked in a slightly croaky and weak voice. His animated face still smiling.

"I'm just trying to get in touch with the gentleman next door actually," the Detective responded. "Does he have a white 4x4?"

"Yes," replied the old man, "but please don't ask me what type, they all look the same to me. It has got black windows though at the back."

"And does he live alone or with someone?"

"Alone," responded the old man. "And I've never seen him with visitors. He told me that his family were all abroad. He is quiet and pleasant but quite private," he responded. "Is there a problem?" he asked?

"No sir," answered the Detective, "this is all just routine. He's not at home, so where would he be now?"

"O I don't know," answered the old man. "He sometimes goes away for nights at a time as he seems to like the outdoors. But he has been in most days in the past week or so. His car is probably in the garage. He's been working a little on it. I saw him washing it the other day and he mentioned that he had found some nice, cheap tyres which he had put on. I know it's got very large ones."

The Detective was intrigued. All the pieces appeared to be falling in place and he was becoming increasingly on edge. A quiet, private individual with darkened windows and new tyres. This is exactly what the Priest has indicated and was too much of a coincidence. He had just two more questions as his mind was considering his next move.

"Any children in the house?"

"No, he lives alone," answered the old man. "No animals and no children. Very quiet. Nice neighbour. Not that he has helped us with anything but just a nice decent young man. Probably been in the army."

That was the detective's next question, about the fatigues. But he stayed quiet as his training had taught him to ask and then allow people to speak and to listen attentively.

The old man continued, "Because he wears that army uniform sometimes, for his trousers anyway."

"Thank-you," answered the Detective. "Please don't worry, this is all routine."

"No it isn't," the old man responded. No one comes here asking these questions. "What do you think he's done? Are we safe?"

"I really can't discuss it," replied the Detective, "probably nothing, but thank-you again."

With that the permanently smiling old man closed the door but continued to look through his window to see what was going on.

The Detective couldn't wait. He went again to the suspect's house and took out his skeleton keys to try and open the front door. No luck there. He then went around the back and tried the back door. The garden was mostly paved with a few oddly shaped trees. Minimum maintenance.

Success. He opened it quietly and crept in. Although there had been no answer, the owner may have been sleeping so he needed to go carefully and quietly. His heightened senses on full alert. He was in a dirty and smelly kitchen. Old plates, bits of food. Pretty disgusting but no sign of mould so not abandoned. There was evidence of a meal the night before and scraps of food on the floor. He couldn't work out if there were two people eating or just one. He proceeded to the hall way. Empty, dull and boring. The back room was dark with its curtains drawn. Just furnished with a table, computer and a sofa. Magazines piled up on the table. A quick glance showed they were a mixture of combat, filthy porn and outdoor lifestyles. The front room appeared to be a TV lounge. A large flat screen on the wall, sloping slightly and with untidy wires protruding from the back. More piles of magazines and a sofa set with the remotes on the glass table in front of the main sofa. Pretty basic and functional. Now upstairs.

He climbed the stairs very slowly trying to be as quiet as possible. They creaked but his adrenalin was pumping and he was committed to find this young girl. When he reached the top of the stairs he saw four doors leading off the small landing. Two of them were closed. He quickly assessed that the bathroom door was closed along with the front main bedroom door. He would try that door first. On full alert and being as quiet as possible, he pressed the handle very slowly and opened it, stepping inside and ready for anything. The curtains were drawn and the bed was messy. It smelled a bit stuffy but it was empty. Only the main bedroom had its curtains drawn. All other rooms also empty of people but full of stuff. Suitcase, boxes, broken electrical items. The bathroom was also not very clean but its small window was open providing some relief.

Nothing upstairs. Just used for sleeping and storage. He also noticed some clothes and a number of files. Nothing illegal and nothing indicating any foul play. As he looked through some of the things, he was constantly on alert to the sound of a car outside. Then he froze as he saw a small teddy. 'This was the house', he thought. 'This is the place.' He decided to call it in and got on his mobile phone. Although the house was empty, he was still whispering. His commander agreed with him and would send officers to assist. He would also contact vehicle patrols for the 4x4 as they had the registration and it needed to be stopped and searched and the driver apprehended.

With the phone call over the Detective decided to leave and wait in his car, although he would check out the garage first. There was a side door from the hallway. He slowly descended the stairs and opened the garage door, looking inside for the light switch. He found it and switched it on. Two tube lights flickered and then started illuminating the garage. It was bare except for a few car tools, car parts, an old bonnet and various household items. Also some camping gear piled into one of the corners. No vehicle. However, there was a chest freezer at the other end of the garage. The Detective paused. He didn't want to look inside but he had to. Now help was on its way, he felt a bit safer. He walked towards it and prayed. He opened it and looked inside. The light was not working so he took out his small torch and shone it inside. There was a huge build up of ice on all sides of the freezer and a few brown, frozen boxes. He moved some of them around with one hand and saw a heavy duty plastic bag with its end tied into a massive knot. He tried to move it and put his torch in his mouth so that he could use both hands. It was heavy and didn't budge. 'No,' he thought. 'No it can't be.' He was looking down at the back of a young person's frozen head, just visible through the clouded plastic. A white and frosted head through the bag could be clearly made out. It looked like she was in the foetal position and possibly tied. Difficult to move but it was definitely not an animal. It was a human head with long human hair.

The Detective was deeply shocked and he almost dropped his torch. It was surreal and it was completely unexpected. Suddenly a loud motor switched on as the automatic garage door began to open and the suns light suddenly invaded the garage, rapidly spreading across the floor. The detective was startled as he turned around with the torch still in his mouth. Should he run or stay? He turned and faced the opening door, turning his torch off and frantically putting it into his pocket. He squinted at the bright sunshine. The freezer was directly opposite the main garage door in the corner farthest from the interconnecting door.

The main door was opening fast and noisily. It was now too late to run as in front of him was the white 4x4 with darkened windows, partially turned ready to drive in. A giant and powerful V8 engine throbbed noisily with the sound magnified in the small garage, echoing off the walls. Its protruding silver bull bars boasting size, power and strength. This beast of the road was silhouetted against a clear, bright, blue summer sky. The Detective stood fully upright and expected the driver to reverse and drive off. What he did though was unexpected. The driver saw the Detective in front of him and the opened freezer directly behind. With little hesitation he pressed down on his accelerator as hard as he could and drove at full acceleration forward. The engine let out a deep, deafening roar as it growled and exploded into life with all its eight pistons firing. 390 horsepower unleashed themselves in a split second as the rear wheels skidded into life accelerating this mechanical monster forward. The Detective ran to the side door as fast as he could but the driver swerved to his left to make sure he hit him. And hit him he did. A loud and prolonged crashing noise echoed around the small garage as the vehicle drove into the Detective, bashing into his torso against the rear wall as his head smashed and cracked open on the solid bonnet. Just a weak, helpless crash dummy in front of this V8 animal. His waist was pinned against the wall as he groaned with pain. Then the noise of a few items falling to the floor, clinking and rolling as the engine went into a deep idle.

The driver then calmly selected reverse and backed away, watching the Detective sliding off and dropping into a slump onto the floor. A trail of blood traced out on the bonnet. The driver then slowly placed the automatic into first and drove into his twitching, broken body a second time just to be sure. Only then did he drive off, closing the garage door behind him remotely, leaving the young Detective for dead. All was quiet in the garage as the Detectives blood oozed out, pooling onto the dirty, concrete garage floor as he quickly lost consciousness. Meanwhile the sun shone brightly outside as people enjoyed the beginning of a lovely summer day.

# 23.  Coma

It had all happened instantaneously yet occurred in slow motion.  It did not seem real and appeared to be a distant dream.  Illusory.

But it was real and it was the past.  An ugly, brutal, dirty truth.  The Detective's breathing was steady and the machine calmly registering a regular heartbeat.  Silent and peaceful.  The hospital room was dark and quiet except for a comforting beep from the heart monitor every time his heart pumped.  It was a private room with curtains drawn and lights dimmed.  The night passed and the new dawn broke time after time— the man totally oblivious as the weeks had passed by.  Lying flat and motionless, at the edge of death and the edge of life.

The neighbourly, smiling old man had raised the alarm.  He had also administered some first aid saving the Detectives life.  The 4x4 and driver had been apprehended within a few hours.  His was a different story.  Unspeakable, but part of the sordid truth of the depths of our depravity.  He was unharmed.  Healthy, fit, unremorseful.  The young girl's funeral had also taken place.  The cause of death was strangulation and now a long, drawn out court case was to follow with a lifelong stay at the tax payers' expense.  Not really being punished, rather being kept away from the public.

The Detective had lost a lot of blood in the accident but his coma had slowed his entire system down.  With his serious and severe injuries, all had thought he could not have survived but he did survive.  It was not his time.  His body crushed, some parts beyond recognition. Bones broken, limbs twisted and bashed, skull fractured. He was extremely lucky and had somehow clung to life.

In the mornings he was normally alone. In the afternoon his hand was being held by his wife. Exhaustion and acceptance had dried up her tears many weeks before. Qur'anic verses were now playing soothingly in the background. Every now and again she stroked his head and tidied his hair and beard. Her world had collapsed around her after his accident. Doctors had given him only a 20% chance for recovery. But he was alive. His coma was deep and his brain had haemorrhaged in the accident. Blood had been oozing out of his ears in the first few days, being allowed to drip into a cheap, cardboard tray. This precious red nectar now worthless and discarded.

She had faith though. The Priest had given her hope and said the chances of recovery were better than Doctors had indicated. He had written some holy words which she had placed around his neck. As soon has she had done that, his body twitched as if a mild electric shock had passed through it. Then it remained still.

She was also reciting some special, religious words at various times, blowing on him gently after completing them. And for her husband, he sensed impressions and he sensed pain. He felt no need to wake up although he thought he could if he wanted. When she had placed the holy words around his neck, he felt his soul had been jolted by a spiritual defibrillator. He was told to wake up, but a more powerful force compelled him to continue to sleep. So he gave in. But the battle for his consciousness had started and was being waged for him. He would be called soon enough.

Strange noises and experiences. A mix of dulled emotions. He did not feel hungry but felt his body was receiving nourishment. He felt a loving touch every now and again and familiar voices. Strange dreams of houses and garages and large vehicles and skidding and hurting. Sometimes he felt pain, severe headaches and a powerful hurting both in body and in his heart. Usually though a deep, deep sleep. No rush to think or to act. Everything was blunted but everything was fine. A few times a day he had an urge to move his fingers as if he had holy beads in his hand. This was when he dreamed the call to prayer was being made. At this time, his wife used to put the *athaan* on, hoping it may wake him as he had always been punctual in his prayer. She had also hoped that with his *taweez*, he would instantly wake up. Her heart raced when his body twitched but then nothing really happened after that and the dream was forgotten. She would need to find even more patience from the invisible pot of patience inside everyone.

The waking time though was fast approaching. The spiritual medicine had started a slow chain reaction that was reaching its climax. This would in turn activate certain enzymes in the body to allow his transition from his dulled existence to being in a semi-wakeful state. And then the recovery could truly begin. The coma was designed as a safety feature, whether to prepare for life or prepare for death - both for the patient and for those around them. It is a protection mode for the body and the brain, directing it to a safe reality away from the trauma of normal living. It is a defensive shield and a stepping stone into another world. A beckoning and calling which in this case would not be answered as it was not his time.

His breathing began to increase at times, showing an urgency and then back to normal. His heart rate also hurried but then relaxed back to its norm. His mind and body were being prepared for his awakening. And then it happened, without warning and without ceremony.

He slowly opened his eyes. Blinking a few times in the process. This was his door opening back into this life that his brain had tried so hard to protect him from. The *taweez* guiding him back. He tried to move his head but failed. He felt pain and a bitter taste in his mouth. His arms and legs twitched as he attempted to calibrate his thinking and reconnect his brain to his body. What was happening? His head heavy and thinking dulled. He tried to speak but nothing. Over the next few minutes his brain began to sharpen. Just enough to get him thinking some more.

Where was he? What had happened? Why the pain? Why the lack of movement? Why so weak and fragile? Why so warm and why such a darkened room? Why was his wife there, reading?

His wife heard a movement and she instinctively looked down at his head. She breathed in sharply and then let out a quiet gasp. This then turned into a scream as she shouted for the nurse. She could see his eyes struggling and his arm contracting, trying to move. She ran to the door and again shouted for the nurse who heard the panic in her voice and came running. The nurse looked at the patient and saw for herself. She quickly went to work. She made sure he was breathing and all the drips were in order and functioning. She had a quick glance at the monitors and noted that all the readings suggested he was not in his deep sleep any longer.

"Looks like he's waking up!" she said fast and excitedly. "Can you hear me? Wake up!" she shouted at the patient in an uncharacteristically raised voice. His weary and watery eyes slowly turned to the nurse and then to his wife, looking dazed and cloudy. He was still struggling to keep them open, but keep them open he must and keep them open he will. Now was his time. She shouted again and he tried to say something but it came out like a groan, with his mouth trying to move, for the first time in many weeks. It felt dry and bitter. She turned his head to the side to ensure that he would not choke if he suddenly vomited. He groaned again as his eyes looked at his wife. It had begun. The revival. The second chance.

Death only occurs if it's written. All have to die but for this Detective, he would be required to endure many more years of this short and troubled life. Death was indeed written for him, but not written for him today.

# 24. Origins

"So what do you do?" asked the Priest.

The young woman was sitting in-front of him along with her husband. Very shy and not eager to talk. So a little small talk was required to try and relax everyone.

This couple had a very weird and interesting problem. They had already been to see medical specialists, Pakistani herbalists and Chinese acupuncturists and other spiritual Priests but to no avail. Much money had been spent and much time wasted. Now they had heard of this Priest and despite reservations from their family, they decided to 'try him out'.

She began with a slightly shaky voice. "Actually, I'm a writer. I've written two light-hearted and entertaining books on the origin of 'things'.

"What are these 'things' please?" asked the Priest?

"Well," she replied, "these 'things' are words and well known actions in life."

The Priest was interested and asked for examples, which she gave happily as she settled into this meeting. The summer was ending and it was cooling down. Days were getting shorter and autumn was waiting to spring. The husband was quiet, calm and dressed in a simple nylon trousers and warm cotton shirt. Looking sophisticated and professional. The wife in a light jacket, dark headscarf and jeans, looking also looking professional. Both wore matching colours, which looked a bit weird.

"For example, she began, 'saluting'. When in the military or police forces, why do people salute?"

"That's a nice question," the Priest responded.

"Yes," she said, "and the answer is very interesting. It goes back to the Knights on horses in their suits of armour. After a demonstration or victory in a tournament, the knights used to parade in front of the king and as a show of respect to the king and dignitaries, when they marched past they used to lift their visors to show their faces – and the practice continues today, but without the visor. Saluting!"

The Priest was impressed. He had learned something. Not something to be used usefully, but a connection with the past that allowed him to appreciate the present.

"That's very interesting," he encouraged. How about food. Do you know for example, where.... biscuits come from?" Biscuits were chosen as they were present on a plate in front of them.

"Yes," she answered, "they were actually used by sailors as a way to preserve non-perishable, dried food items for their long journeys for nourishment. A biscuit form provided a healthy mix in a convenient shape for both eating and storage. Now of course, they have become a comfort and luxury food. A delicacy rather than a life-saving food item as it was then."

"And you have put all of these in a book?" enquired the Priest.

"Yes," she replied. "Actually, two books. The first was called 'Black and White', and the second is called 'A Light Touch'."

"Nice names," said the Priest with a smile. He had begun writing something on his pad in front of him as he knew she had settled down so had begun the treatment.

"Please," he said softly, "please continue."

"Well," she started, "do you know where pole-vaulting came from?"

"No," responded the Priest. "It's quite a strange sport to exist I suppose, let alone having survived from the past."

"You are right," she said. "But when you realise where it came from, you will appreciate why and how it exists. If you think about it, long poles like this have only really been used for canal boating. So now we know what they were used for, how come people use them for jumping over a bar? Well, the boatmen used to jump from one bank of the canal to another using these poles. Gradually a competition started amongst the boatmen and we are where we are."

"Fascinating," said the Priest. "I never knew that."

"Yes," she continued, "and just to bring this subject up to date, if I could mention 'computer bug' and explain why it is called a 'bug'."

"Yes," said the husband all of a sudden. "I've always wondered that." As he was a self-taught computer expert and even did some programming in his spare time, so he sat up a bit, never really in the past paying much attention to his wife's interest.

"Well," she continued, "you have to appreciate that computers of the past were made from valves and wires rather than microchips, and reprogramming was by changing the wires around in the large computer cabinet. So, when once it didn't work, the engineers searched the valves and wires and found a dead moth in the system. This they called a 'bug' and the name stuck."

"Wow," said her husband, "I never knew that. That's really interesting."

"Yes, " said the Priest, "please continue."

Now she was very comfortable and realised what the Priest was all about. A sincere, gentle, father-like figure who was there to help. The aura in his office and is own persona all indicated that he could solve their problem and possibly he was one of a very few people living who could solve it.

"Well, saying 'cheers' and hitting glasses together came about form the Vikings. They used to make sure their drinks mixed to ensure that no-one had poisoned them. And the some common words, which we use everyday but don't analyse. here is 'hello', 'goodbye' and 'breakfast' for example."

The husband was still in listening mode, but not listening with his brain switched off, as was normal, he was listening with his brain switched on, which was not normal.

"Goodbye is short for 'God be with you', 'hello' was used to draw attention to yourself when on the phone although 'ahoy'

202

was also considered. And 'breakfast' is exactly what it says. One is breaking ones fast after spending all night not eating: break- fast."

There was quiet in the room as the husband absorbed the simple and obvious analysis. The Priest continued to write.

The couple were curious what he was writing but were too polite to ask.

"You are probably wondering what I'm writing," he asked. There was polite silence as to admit this would be impolite and to deny it would be an untruth.

The Priest smiled and looked at both of them. They were courteous and quiet. Tired after seeking so much help from so many people and with no result. Lots of promises and no solutions. However, there was a little hope here. A small light in the gloomy darkness.

"Well," he continued, "I am hopefully writing a solution for you."

There was no reaction from the couple. They were both listening.

"But we haven't told you our problem," said the husband.

"Well," answered the Priest, "I think looking at you both, I think I know what it is."

Now they were looking surprised and they had awakened from their deafness and were looking at the Priest with wide-open eyes and a slight disbelief.

"So..., " began the husband, "could you tell us what it is please?"

The Priest breathed in and sat back. He smiled a little and then made a comment that startled both of them. "Your problem," he began, "is that one of you is being deceptive. One of you is not human."

Both had the look of shock and horror on their faces as they looked at each other and then looked at the Priest.

# 25. The Final Test

The student had been summoned. Rarely this happened, but the Priest was sick and in bed for a number of days. He had told very few about his circumstances and had been helping people on the phone rather than in person. His visits had also been reducing over the previous year and his student had been shadowing him for the past few months. He quietly walked into the house, greeted its occupants in his usual modest and humble manner and then went to the Priests private rest room.

The Priest glanced up at the student, whom, with great love and affection gently took the Priest's hand and kissed it. He then sat on the floor as the Priest slowly and painfully sat up in his bed. The room smelt sweet and fragrant and the Priest, despite looking tired and weak, was radiant.

"I am grateful you could come," he said, pausing for breath. "I would just like to inform you that you are about to face your final test." Then another short breather. "It will probably be the most challenging one as it will last your entire life. I also want to tell you that you will pass this test ... *inshaAllah*. And I will be with you... always."

With that the Priest sank back into his pillow, tired and still struggling to breathe. His condition had deteriorated rapidly in the past week and this sudden meeting was unexpected. There was a long silence as all that had to be said had been said. Tears welled inside the students eyes and were released into the world where they belonged. The Priest's eyes also moist and glistening, still struggling with his breathing. The student was devastated. He looked at his mentor who looked very sick and semi-conscious. The Student was profoundly sad, broken-hearted and was now uncontrolled in his crying. Deep down though he understood. Their souls were connected through their hearts and he knew full well what the Priest meant and he knew full well that the Priest was right.

A new test for this young Apprentice and a new beginning.

## 26.  A New Beginning

The Angel slowly approached and waited just above the Priest's blessed head.  Perfectly poised, majestic and exceptionally beautiful in appearance and in expression.  The Priest could see his spiritual beauty in its entirety, in this world and the next.  Comfortably and peacefully the Angel's handsome and radiant face with glistening eyes looked at this noble man with delight and admiration.  His torturous worldly pain was now subsiding.  He was experiencing both worlds but his worldly life was ebbing away into a different existence.  There was no resistance, only comfort and joy, immense peace and a tremendous tranquillity.

Then the Angel spoke in his adorable, serene and alluring voice.  "Welcome..... O noble and beautiful soul... most welcome."  And he breathed his last and smiled his lasting smile.

* * * * * * * * * *

# Glossary

| | |
|---|---|
| Alhamdulillah | Praise be to Allah |
| Ameen | Amen (may it be so) |
| Assalmu alaikum | Peace be to you |
| Athaan | Call to prayer |
| Awliyaa | Friends (of Allah) |
| Babba | Old man |
| Badtameez bacha | Extremely disrespectful boy |
| Biryani | Rice and meat dish |
| Bismillah | In the name of God |
| Du'a | Supplication |
| Dupatta | Scarf |
| Hazrat | Honorary |
| Haqq | Truth / reality |
| 'Ibadah | Worship |
| Iman | Faith |
| Ihsan | Extremely strong faith |
| Insha Allah | God-willing |
| Jinn | Another form of life |
| Kameez | Traditional trousers |
| Masha Allah | As God wills |
| Musalla | Prayer mat |
| Naan | Bread |
| Nafs | Self, ego, psyche |
| Rahmatulla alaih | Mercy of Allah upon him |
| Sajdah | Prostration |
| Salaams | Prayers of peace |
| Shaikh | Guide |
| Takbir | Allah is Great |
| Tamasha | Hullaballoo |
| Taweez | Holy words on small paper |
| Thumma amen | Again, amen |

# Dedication

This book and the stories therein are dedicated to the memory and great work of Hazrat Allama Peer Muhammad Abdul Wahab Siddiqi (*rahmatulla alaih*). Along with true *awliyaa* of the past, his special life and guidance embodies all that is good, pure and precious.

Those who met him are truly fortunate and those who have learned from him are blessed. He wished only to do good and dedicated his life as such, inspiring the hearts of every soul he encountered.

His beautiful life story cannot be told in mere words but the changes he transformed are testament to his sweetness, strength and spirituality.

The knowledge he imparted, his clarity of thought and expression, his teachings and inspiring personality still benefit us today.

A truly remarkable individual who made life and its tests special, bearable and defeatable. May we continue to benefit from his beautiful wisdom, vision and dedication. His tremendous work he undertook whilst on the earth - he continues to undertake.

Thus this book is dedicated to those who serve.

www.spiritpriest.com

# About the Author

Shaikh Tauqir Ishaq is an international lecturer in Islamic Sciences and has authored a number of scientific papers, novels and reference books. He has lectured and written on a variety of subjects including *Fiqh*, *Hadith*, *Tafseer*, *Aqeeda*, Science and Islam and *Tasawwuf*.

He has learned spirituality (*tasawwuf*) from the masters and wishes to share some of his experiences and insights into this beautiful and amazing world.

It is hoped that this book provides as many questions as answers as through such ways knowledge is gained and appreciated.

Our essence is our soul and we need to understand and we can only benefit from our spirituality if we are able to better ourselves and help those around us.

Spirituality permeates our very being, our character , our pre-lives, current lives, our deaths and afterlife. It is a subject about which much is written and but most is misunderstood.

If we deny our spirituality then we corrupt ourselves. We are our soul and our soul is us for as long as we exist.

Please read, enjoy and be inspired...

www.spiritpriest.com